*"Don't be frightened of
the storm, Billie,"
he said softly.*

"I'm not going to let you go through this scared out of your mind."

"But I'm not—" She started to protest but was interrupted by his low, mischievous chuckle.

"I believe I've come up with something that may help," he drawled. "I've always thought that actions speak louder than words." He slowly shifted his body to nestle comfortably in the cradle of her hips as if he'd found a home. "Suppose you think of this instead of what's going on around us."

Billie inhaled sharply. "For heaven's sake, we're practially at death's door, and I'm not even sexy!"

"You're not? You could have fooled me." His teeth nibbled delicately at the lobe of her ear and she felt a thrill of heat start somewhere in the pit of her stomach. "Don't worry, love. I'm not going to rush you into anything. But I do want you. Now you just lie here and think about how much I want you and all the delicious things I'd like to do to you. I'll even whisper a few of them to you from time to time. Try to think about that instead of the storm."

Try? She found it difficult to think of anything else, conscious only of the warm heat of his body against hers. . . .

WHAT ARE *LOVESWEPT* ROMANCES?

They are stories of true romance and touching emotion. We believe those two very important ingredients are constants in our highly sensual and very believable stories in the *LOVESWEPT* line. Our goal is to give you, the reader, stories of consistently high quality that may sometimes make you laugh, sometimes make you cry, but are always fresh and creative and contain many delightful surprises within their pages.

Most romance fans read an enormous number of books. Those they truly love, they keep. Others may be traded with friends and soon forgotten. We hope that each *LOVESWEPT* romance will be a treasure—a "keeper." We will always try to publish

LOVE STORIES YOU'LL NEVER FORGET
BY AUTHORS YOU'LL ALWAYS REMEMBER

The Editors

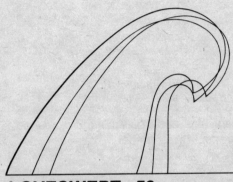

LOVESWEPT • 59

Iris Johansen
Touch the Horizon

BANTAM BOOKS
TORONTO • NEW YORK • LONDON • SYDNEY • AUCKLAND

TOUCH THE HORIZON
A Bantam Book / September 1984

Words and Music to See You Shine by Roger Whittaker,
Tembo Album TMT-3778 © 1980,
Tembo Music, Canada (CAPAC). Used by Permission.
All Rights Reserved.

ISBN 0-553-21665-1

Published simultaneously in the United States and Canada

Bantam Books are published by Bantam Books, Inc. Its
trademark, consisting of the words "Bantam Books" and the
portrayal of a rooster, is Registered in U.S. Patent and Trademark Office and in other countries. Marca Registrada. Bantam
Books, Inc., 666 Fifth Avenue, New York, New York 10103.

PRINTED IN THE UNITED STATES OF AMERICA

O   0 9 8 7 6 5 4 3 2 1

One

Shades of Lawrence of Arabia, Billie Callahan thought in stunned amazement: The prince of the desert was a golden man! She impatiently brushed strands of copper-colored hair away from her face, her eyes intent on the rider on the black Arabian stallion galloping toward her over the dunes. Her hair whipped again around her face, stinging her cheeks. The wind was definitely rising, and, standing on the top of a tiny hill, she was exposed to its full force. It seemed now to attack her clothing as well, snatching at her shirt and pants like a starving animal who'd cornered its prey and couldn't wait to devour it.

When the Jeep had conked out a short way down the road, she'd thought it would be a good idea to climb the little hill to see if she could determine how far she'd have to walk to reach Zalandan. Now she wasn't at all sure it had been such a good idea. She felt very vulnerable on this lonely promontory, and the sight that met her eyes wasn't all that reassuring. Golden sand dunes rolled for miles to merge with the rapidly darkening skyline. A flash of lightning illuminated the cliffs on the horizon, but they seemed so terribly far away. Beyond those cliffs lay the safety of the city of Zalandan, Yusef had told her, but she'd never make it there before the storm struck in force. The wind lifted and swirled the sand in wild, ghostly patterns, the crests of the dunes moving like whirling dervishes.

She'd better try to get back to the Jeep and the slight protection it offered. She took a last curious glance at the rider on the black Arabian stallion before she turned and started down the hill. She'd first seen him as a blurred figure on the horizon. Despite the predicament she found herself in, the sight of him caught at her imagination.

Dressed in a white flowing burnoose that contrasted dramatically with the lustrous black coat of the horse, he looked graceful and dynamic. A prince of the desert from one of those old forties technicolor epics, she'd thought bemusedly. All he needed was a sword and a harem girl thrown across the bow of his saddle to complete the fantasy image. He came from the direction of the cliffs and probably was a resident of Zalandan, but he had all the dash of a desert brigand or a bedouin sheikh rather than a city dweller. And that was why she'd been startled when he'd come close enough for her to see his coloring. His hair wasn't raven-black, as she'd expected, but a dark gold burnished by the sun. In the few months she'd been in Sedikhan, she'd never seen a blond native of this Mideastern country. Yet native he must be, judging by that flowing burnoose, and particularly by the way he managed the stallion.

Well, whoever he was, she mustn't expect help from him, she thought with a shrug. He probably wasn't headed in her direction anyway. Undoubtedly he would swerve to take the road leading to Yusef's village, some thirty miles across the shifting dunes. Even if she was the rider's objective, he might be more of a threat than a help. No, she couldn't count on anyone but herself. But, then, when had she ever wanted it any other way? She'd weathered many a storm, both mental and physical, and she'd overcome this one too.

She reached the bottom of the hill and fought to keep her footing. The gusts seemed to try to lift and sweep her away as if she were just another of the millions of grains of sand they dominated so easily. The sand stung her cheeks now, and she closed her eyes to keep out the sharp particles swirling all around her.

"What the devil are you doing out here in the middle of nowhere?" The voice was rough and masculine, and she opened her eyes to see her desert prince slipping lithely out of the saddle only a few yards from her. The wind was shrieking so loudly that she hadn't even heard the sound of hoofbeats. He was no native . . . and he certainly wasn't Lawrence of Arabia. That drawl sounded more like Texas than Oxford.

"What does it look like I'm doing?" she asked crossly, shouting to be heard over the wind. "I've been told there's nothing better for the complexion than a sandstorm, so I thought I'd drive out in the middle of one and try it." She found her voice was quavering with nervousness, and it only increased her annoyance. "I'm trying to stay alive, dammit!"

The wind whipped that golden hair about his face as it tore at her.

"You're not doing too good a job," he said grimly, as he came toward her. "In a few minutes this is going to escalate into a full-fledged storm, and you're wandering around as if you were at a garden party." He grabbed her elbow. "Come on, we've got to get to shelter."

"That's where I was going," she said indignantly as he hustled her briskly toward a cluster of rocks while leading the black behind them. "I was heading toward my Jeep to wait out the storm."

"Unless it's only a few yards away you'd never have made it," he said tersely. "You'd probably have wandered away from the road and smothered to death within ten minutes."

She felt a shiver run through her that she tried to mask with a light laugh. "Nonsense. I have a wonderful sense of direction. I'd have made it."

"I'm glad you're so confident." He pushed her behind the sheltering rocks that were barely waist-high. "Stay there while I take care of old Nick, here." He led the horse toward another cluster of rocks nearby.

Billie sank down into the shelter of the boulders and suddenly felt very alone and afraid. How stupid to be so scared; soon the storm would be over and she would have survived it, as she had all the others in her life.

A white blur appeared through the curtain of sand that enveloped her, and the golden-haired desert man dropped down beside her. "It's not too bad here yet, but the wind is picking up steadily. We're going to get the brunt of it any time now."

Her violet eyes widened apprehensively. "It's going to get worse?" How could it get any worse, when the world already seemed to be splitting open and releasing all the gibbering fiends of hell? She drew a deep breath and said with forced lightness, "Well, it probably won't be all that bad. We have the base of the hill on one side and a humongous rock on the other to protect us."

"Don't kid yourself," he said as he drew the loose hood of the burnoose over his hair. "I've seen storms like this shift tons of sand and completely rearrange the landscape. An hour from now there could be a twenty-foot dune where we're sitting."

"Do you have to be so reassuring?" she asked ironically. "You wouldn't want me to get *too* cocky about our chances for survival."

"We'll survive," he said absently. "Lie down."

"What?" she asked, startled.

"Lie down. I'm going to cover you with my body. The burnoose will give us both a small measure of protection. Not much, but we need every edge we can get."

"But I don't—"

He didn't wait for her to finish, and she suddenly found herself flat on her back in the sand with him astride her. He parted the robe to reveal a soft white shirt tucked into low-slung, faded jeans. Definitely not Lawrence of Arabia, she thought hazily. Then he lowered his body on top of hers and she found that she couldn't think at all. She could feel the warm heat of his body through the material of the clothing that separated them, and it came as a little shock. He was resting his weight on his knees and elbows on each side of her, but she could feel every line of his lean, muscular body with a detailed intimacy that made her oddly breathless. Her face was pressed into the soft white shirt, and she was aware of a faint lemony scent blended with the clean smell of soap and the tangy musk odor of the virile male.

"I don't think this is really necessary," she said faintly.

He lifted himself a little to look down at her, and she got another shock that was almost as great as the touch of his body. Good Lord, he was beautiful! She hadn't been conscious of anything but that golden hair and deep, vibrant voice in the swirling mist of sand that had surrounded them, since he'd appeared beside her. Now there were only a few inches between them, and she knew she'd never seen a more beautiful human being before in her life. His finely molded bone structure was almost classical, and the golden bronze of his skin shone like the patina on a statue that might have graced the Acropolis. Still, there was nothing in the least hard or rigid in the sensual curve of his lips, and his eyes were the clearest, deepest blue she'd ever seen. She'd always thought blue eyes were a little cold, but now she realized they could be as warm as the first breath of spring. Warm and understanding and wise. Wise? What a strange adjective to come to mind in connection with an explosively virile man who couldn't be older than his late twenties. Yet there was a gentle wisdom in the depths of those eyes that went far beyond intelligence and might have belonged to a man in the twilight of his life.

"It's necessary."

"What?" She had forgotten the protest she'd made a moment before, and she hastily pulled her attention from those wise, clear eyes and that beautifully sensual mouth to the matter at hand. "You can't be very comfortable. If you'll just let me up, I'll be quite all right."

"Shhh." He smiled down at her, and the smile lit his face with such gentle glowing warmth that she felt a strange unfolding deep inside her. "Relax, windflower. I know how strong and sturdy you are. You won't lose any of that strength by letting me shelter you for a few minutes. I only want to keep your pretty petals from being hurt and torn."

The wind howled like a lost soul now. The sheets of sand around them seemed to be thickening, and she felt a swift rush of panic. "That's all very poetic," she said shakily. "I don't think I've ever had anyone compare me to a flower before. Certainly not when we were both about to be smothered to death."

Tiny lines appeared at the corner of his eyes as he grinned down at her. "But you are like a windflower. I thought so the minute I saw you standing on the top of that hill with the wind tearing at those bright, shining curls and whipping at your delicate body. You remind me a little of a chrysanthemum, but there's more strength and endurance in you than they have. Yes, you're definitely a windflower." Then his eyes narrowed on her face, which was showing more strain each moment. "You're really frightened, aren't you? I thought you were joking, but I can feel you trembling against me."

"No," she denied quickly. "I'm not afraid. It's just that I've never been in a sandstorm before and I don't know what to expect." She made a conscious effort to still the quaking that had betrayed her, but she found to her disgust that it couldn't be done. "Just give me a minute and I'll be—"

"I'll give you all the time you need, windflower," he interrupted gently. "And you shouldn't be ashamed of being afraid. We're all afraid at some time or other. I was scared to death myself when I saw the wind trying to push you off the top of the hill. I wasn't sure you had the strength to fight it, and I was so far away I wouldn't have had time to get to you if you hadn't." He spread the folds of his burnoose so that it covered her like a sheet, and his hard, smooth cheek was suddenly against her own. The loose hood that covered his head now covered hers as well, and she felt wrapped in a dark cocoon of security. "You're not going to die, windflower. Not for a long, long time, and when you do I'll be there holding you just like this." His voice was a deep velvet murmur in her hair, and she felt almost mesmerized by the intimate darkness, the tactile warmth and fragrance that was being woven about her senses. "We're going to get through this together. Forget about the wind, the sand, the storm. Just think of the two of us lying here giving our strength to each other. Do you know how wonderful that sharing can be? Two people able to reach out and touch each other, helping each other to climb. Think about that instead."

She did think about it and, oh, how like a lovely dream it was. His body on hers felt as familiar as if they'd lain like this a thousand times before; his intimate words had the same odd familiarity. Intimate? She felt a tiny shock zing through the velvet that encircled them. This wasn't only intimacy, a virile male making a move on an available, not unattractive woman. This stranger was making *love* to her with words, and that was totally insane.

"This is crazy," she said dazedly, trying to stiffen against him. The action only brought her in closer contact with the hard warmth of the body that she was finding so exciting. She decided she was better off lying pliant and unresisting. "*You're* crazy. I don't want you to say things like that."

"Are you feeling threatened?" he asked tenderly. His lips moved against her temple in the most delicate of gossamer kisses. "All right, I'll back off, windflower. If I can't take your mind off your nervousness one way, I'll have to take another approach. Talk to me. What's your name?"

Windflower. The word zoomed out of the jumble of emotions cascading through her. "Billie Callahan, and I'm *not* nervous."

His chuckle was like warm velvet against her forehead. "Right, of course you're not. What are you doing out here in the middle of the Sedikhan desert, Billie Callahan?"

"I was on my way to Zalandan when my Jeep broke down. I've been visiting for the last few days in a small village about fifteen miles from here."

"Visiting who?" An edge of sharpness was just barely discernible beneath the velvet.

"Yusef Ibraheim and his family." She made a face he couldn't see because of their closeness, but he caught the ruefulness in her voice. "Yusef and I have been something of a matched set for the last few weeks, and I thought it would be a good idea to take him home and deposit him with his family."

"He's your lover?" The sharpness had cut through the velvet now, and it startled her.

"Heavens, no! I just did him a favor once, and Yusef seems to have some wildly antiquated ideas about his obligations in regard to returning that favor." There was a thread of exasperation in her voice. "Besides, he has this crazy idea I need someone to take care of me, and he's elected himself to do it. I thought returning him to his family would make him forget all about me. It didn't work, so I took off for Zalandan on my own in the middle of the night."

"I see." His tone was solemn, but she could detect a note of underlying amusement that annoyed her exceedingly. "I don't know why he couldn't understand how totally capable you are of running your own life. I'd be interested to know what experiences triggered a misapprehension like that. You wouldn't care to enlighten me, would you, windflower?"

"Billie," she corrected. She certainly wasn't about to "enlighten" him, she thought crossly. It would make her look like even more of an irresponsible idiot than she did now. Circumstances and her own impulsiveness seemed constantly to conspire to project that image anyway. "It doesn't matter, does it? We don't even know each other. You couldn't possibly be interested."

"Oh, I'm interested, all right," he said. " 'Intrigued' is more the word. But then, I knew the first time I caught sight of you that you were going to be a constant source of delight and fascination to me. If you won't go into your adventures with Yusef, perhaps you'll tell me what you're doing in Sedikhan. We don't get too many Americans here other than oil technicians. Do you work for one of the oil companies?"

That was a reasonable assumption, since Sedikhan was one of the richest oil kingdoms in the world. She suddenly wished she could have answered in the affirmative. It sounded so sensible, and doubtless would have improved her credibility. "No, I came to Sedikhan to play a featured role in *Desert Venture*, an adventure movie that was filmed partially in a village on the outskirts of Marasef."

"You're an actress?"

The incredulity in his voice caused her to bristle.

"I did very well for a first role. My director said so."
Then she added with reluctant honesty, "Well,
that's not quite true. He said I was very effective,
which is a different thing entirely. We both knew I
was a lousy actress, but he didn't care as long as I
looked vulnerable and wistful. It was the expression on my face he wanted, not my acting ability."

"I can understand that." He raised his head to
look down into deep violet eyes framed in extrava-
gant lashes; her eyes had the mistiness of a
dreamer of dreams. Hers was not a beautiful face,
but there was something so sensitive and loving in
the curve of those lips and the clear honesty in her
eyes that it tugged at the heart. "I find that I'm
wanting that face very much myself. I want it on
the pillow next to mine and across the breakfast
table and . . ."

"You weren't going to say things like that," she
interjected hurriedly.

"Sorry." He didn't sound at all apologetic. "Go
on. You were saying that you were a lousy actress?"

"Terrible. But it didn't make any difference,
because this is probably the only film I'll be in anyway. I only accepted the role because it was a
chance to get a free trip to Sedikhan. I like to visit
new places."

"Windflower." This time his tone was thoughtful. "But even windflowers have roots. What are
yours, Billie? A family, a special place?"

"I'm an orphanage brat," she said lightly. "And
all places are special in their own way. And I can't
possibly be a windflower, because I don't have any
roots. I'm a gypsy, and I'll probably still be one
when I'm ninety. I like my life very much just the
way it is."

"You don't have to be so forceful about it. No

one's arguing with you. We all have to be what we are. I don't want to change you, Billie; that would be altering the natural order of things." He rubbed his cheek lightly, almost teasingly, against hers. "But it's not unnatural to blossom and develop into all you can be. That can be very beautiful. I'd like to watch that happening to you, windflower."

"You're absolutely unbelievable," Billie said blankly. "I've never known anyone to speak to a complete stranger the way you do. Windflowers and blossoms and philosophy. Are you always like this?"

"Most of the time," he said simply. "Something happened to me quite a few years ago that burned all the small talk out of me. Now I don't even try to play word games. Life is too short for us not to be completely honest with one another."

"That could be very dangerous," Billie said slowly. "The world can be a very devious place, and complete honesty leaves you terribly open to hurt."

"It also leaves you open to beauty and truth and the lovely rhythms of life," he said quietly. "And to the knowledge of gypsies like Billie Callahan."

"Knowledge?"

"I'm hoping that if I leave myself open you'll want to come near and give a little of yourself to me. Rest against me and let me learn you. Do you suppose that's possible?"

In that moment she could believe anything was possible with this eccentric man whose voice was mellow as honey and whose words glittered clear as crystal yet bewildered at the same time. "I have an idea it wouldn't make any difference if I said no. Doesn't the fact that we're complete strangers make any difference to you?"

"Why should it? I've always known what I

wanted. I'd just never found it before I lifted my head and saw a windflower clinging to the top of a hill. *My* windflower."

She stirred uneasily, and he recognized the disturbance for what it was. "All right, I'll be quiet," he said with a chuckle. "I know you're not ready for all this yet." This time she was certain he kissed her temple. "But you've got to admit it's taken your mind off the storm."

It certainly had done that, she realized with astonishment. She'd been more aware of the storm of emotions he was arousing under the flowing burnoose than of the one that was going on around their little cocoon. But now she was conscious that the wind was screaming with a fury that was even greater than before, and she tensed involuntarily.

"Yes, it's getting worse," he said quietly. "I think it will reach its height in a few minutes, and I don't know how long it will last after that." He was fumbling in his pocket and brought out a pristine handkerchief that he spread over the lower half of her face, covering her mouth and nostrils. Lemon again and something a little spicy. "Some of the sand is so fine that it's bound to find its way under this hood. It's important to filter it before it fills your mouth and nostrils."

"What about you?" she asked, concerned.

"I have my own filter," he said, burrowing his face contentedly in the copper curls at her temple. "A soft mop of chrysanthemums, silky and smelling deliciously of Shalimar."

It *was* Shalimar, and it appeared he was suspiciously knowledgeable about scents more sophisticated than those of the flowers his speech was sprinkled with. Well, why shouldn't he be? The man was perfectly gorgeous, and women were probably falling all over him. For some reason she shivered with distaste at the thought, and he stiffened against her.

"You're frightened again," he said with a touch of impatience in his voice. "And you won't let me say any of the things that might distract you. I'll be damned if I'm going to let you go through this scared out of your mind."

"But I wasn't—" she started to protest, but she was interrupted by his low, mischievous chuckle.

"I think I've come up with something that might help," he drawled. "I always have believed actions speak louder than words. Suppose you think of this instead of what's going on around us." He slowly brought his loins down to rub intimately in the cradle of her hips before nestling comfortably as if he'd found a home. "I told you I believed in total honesty whenever possible."

She inhaled sharply. Nothing could be more boldly honest than the hard arousal that was cuddled against her. "But you couldn't," she gasped. "For heaven's sake, we're practically at death's door, and I'm not even sexy!"

"You're not? You could have fooled me." His teeth nibbled delicately at the lobe of her ear, and she felt a thrill of heat start somewhere in the pit of her stomach. "I'm obviously finding you very sexy indeed." He rubbed teasingly against her again. "And I hate to disillusion you, Billie, but I'd probably have an identical reaction if we were on a raft in the Indian Ocean in the middle of a hurricane."

"Perhaps you'd better try to distract me with philosophy and windflowers again," Billie said faintly. "I think it might be safer."

"Too late." He chuckled. "I'm finding this much more entertaining. Don't worry, love, I'm not going to rush you into anything. But I do want you, and it's best you realize that's a part of it too."

"I'm finding it hard to ignore it."

"That's the idea," he said softly in her ear. "Now, you just lie here and think about how much I want you and all the delicious things I'd like to do to you. I'll even whisper a few of them to you from time to time. Try to think about that instead."

Try? She was having difficulty thinking of anything else. She was only conscious of the hard, warm heat of him, the scent of lemon and spice and musk, and his words whispering erotically in her ear. Did men really do those things to women? They sounded *sinfully* kinky spoken in that slow velvet drawl. But exciting! She couldn't deny that he made it all sound breathlessly exciting. Was he putting her on, making up stories to scare away the bogeyman? She almost asked him, but she was half afraid she'd receive that low chuckle of amusement that had become so familiar in answer. No, she'd just lie here and let him tell her his Scheherazadian tales, let his voice flow over her. There was no harm in it, and girls like her who looked more like boys seldom had the opportunity to have a beautiful sheikh croon erotic litanies in their ears. Yes, she would relax and enjoy it. There was no hint of a threat in this strange golden man. She knew with an odd, rocklike certainty that he'd never do anything to her she didn't want, despite the evidence of desire that was so blatant.

She was conscious of an overpowering heat and felt a drop of perspiration appear on the temple pressed to her own. Was it caused by the smothering oppression of the storm or the excitement engendered by the verbal pictures he was drawing for her? She couldn't get her breath, but it could be because of the shocking variation he'd just suggested. No, that one he definitely must have made up, she thought in amusement.

She must have giggled, because she heard his low laugh. "Oh! You like that one? We'll have to try it, then. Though we might have to take some acrobatic training first." The smothering heat increased, and his arms tightened around her. "If you like that one, just wait until you hear the one I've been saving up for the *pièce de résistance*." And the passionate litany went on.

Some of the things he suggested were so outrageous, she could only laugh, and some so arousing that it caused a slow-burning flame in places she'd never even known were erogenous. Either way, they wrapped her in a fascination so intense it actually startled her when he suddenly stopped speaking. She impatiently waited for him to start again and then realized that his body was oddly tense and that he was listening. Listening to what? It was the absence of sound that he'd become conscious of. The wind had stopped!

"The storm's over," he said quietly. He lifted his head, and the deep azure eyes were twinkling. "We can get up now. Disappointing, isn't it? I'd only reached number sixty-two in the *Kama Sutra*. I thought surely I'd have time to go on to a few Japanese and Arabic variations. Oh, well, maybe next time." He lifted his brow quizzically. "Unless you prefer we continue now?"

"No, I believe you've gone quite far enough," she said quickly. Too far for her peace of mind. "I think we'd better get up and see if I can find my Jeep under all this sand."

"If you insist." He sighed. "Close your eyes.

There must be two feet of sand on my back, and when I get up, you're going to get a sand shower."

Then, with some effort, he heaved upward. She barely had time to obey his injunction before she was deluged by a heavy cloud of sand that replaced the hard warmth of his body as he stood up. Despite the handkerchief that still covered her mouth and nose, she found herself choking and coughing. She had a sudden chilling realization of what it would have been like if she hadn't been protected by that strong, lithe body. She hadn't really been aware of how close they'd been to death while he was holding her, distracting her. But he'd been fully aware of the danger, she realized suddenly. It was all there in the sober keenness with which he was surveying the terrain. "We're going to have the devil of a time plowing our way through all this loose sand to get to your Jeep. How far down the road did you leave it?"

She sat up and shook her head like a wet puppy. Sand flew in all directions. Lord, she felt gritty. "About half a mile. But there's no use going back there—I told you it had conked out." She lifted a brow. "Unless you think you can fix it."

"No chance," he said with a grimace. "I don't know enough about the insides of a car to change a spark plug. I just thought you'd want to pick up any valuables before I took you on to Zalandan."

"I don't have anything of real value, but there is something I'd like to bring with me. My guitar."

"An old friend?" he asked understandingly.

She nodded. "An old friend." She got to her feet, her short suede boots sinking to the ankle in the loose sand, which she tried to dust from her jeans and soft tunic top. "Suppose I hike down and get it while you check on your horse. That Arabian looked a little high-strung to me. We'll be lucky if he hasn't run away and left us both to hike to Zalandan."

He shook his head. "I told him to stay," he said simply. "Old Nick and I understand each other. He'll still be there. But you go on anyway. I'll have to take off the cloth I tied over his eyes and nostrils and quiet him down a little before I try leading him through this shifting sand." He strode toward the other cluster of rocks nearby, speaking to her over his shoulder. "We won't be able to ride him before we get to ground that's a hell of a lot firmer than this, or he could break a leg." He disappeared behind the rocks, and she heard a welcoming whinny.

Billie shook her head wonderingly as she carefully started winding her way through the newly formed dunes of loose sand. A man who could command a high-spirited Arabian to stay put through a sandstorm and actually be obeyed was mind-boggling. Come to think of it, though, the feat was no more astounding than the other facets of his character he'd shown her. Why was she even surprised?

The small, open Jeep looked like a beach toy whose child owner had shoveled it full of sand, then forgotten it and wandered away to new amusements. There was a green army duffel bag lying on its side a few yards away from the jeep. In the middle of the road Billie Callahan knelt, cradling a shattered guitar in her arms as if it were a wounded child. She wasn't even aware that she was no longer alone until he spoke from a few yards away.

"Billie." It was only her name, but so full of

understanding and sympathy that it pierced even the numb despair she was feeling. She looked up to see him standing a few yards away, the reins of the black in his hand and all the gentleness in the world in his eyes.

"It wasn't worth much, you know." She could feel the foolish tears brim over and run down her cheeks. She traced one of the many scratches on the guitar's battered surface. "I took it with me everywhere, so it got pretty beat up." She was looking at him without really seeing him. "I bought it for twenty bucks in a pawnshop in Santa Fe. I was only fifteen then, and working at a service station pumping gas. I never wanted anything in my life as much as I wanted that guitar in the pawnshop window." She drew a deep breath and shook her head as if to clear it. "Pretty stupid, huh? It didn't look much better then than it does now."

He knelt across from her now, his eyes holding hers with such tenderness it was almost as if he were holding her in his arms. "Not stupid at all. I grew up on a ranch in the Rio Grande valley, and my mother was addicted to books about the West. I remember I once read an old one by Harold Bell Wright about a tenderfoot from the East who wanted to start a new life out west with a brand-new name." He tucked a copper strand of hair gently behind her ear. "Do you know what name he chose? He called himself after a pair of torn and scuffed chaps. He called himself Honorable Patches. He knew it would cause him all kinds of trouble in the wild, woolly West, but he did it anyway. He did it because it signified all the worth and dignity and usefulness he wanted in his life." His index finger gently traced the same scratch on the guitar her own had, while his eyes steadily held hers. "Honorable Patches, Billie."

"Honorable Patches," she echoed, and suddenly felt a healing serenity flood her that miraculously eased her pain. It was as if those glowing eyes were giving her more strength and love and tranquility with every passing second.

She pulled her glance away as she reached for the hunter-green felt case and carefully zipped the shattered guitar within its protective folds. This encounter was growing more weird by the minute, and she felt a sudden desire to edge away from him, from the closeness he was forcing upon her by the very strength of the emotions he was arousing. "It must have been some storm to lift all these things out of the Jeep and toss them around so." She didn't look at him as she rose to her feet and carried the guitar to the Jeep to place it carefully on the back seat. "I guess I'm ready to go. We can't possibly handle the duffel bag on horseback, so I suppose I'll have to wait and have it brought in with the Jeep." She looked over her shoulder with an impish grin. "I trust there's a Triple A in Zalandan. If not, my towing premium is going to be completely wasted."

"I'm afraid you're out of luck." He was picking up the duffel and storing it back in the Jeep. "But we have several cars in the Casbah and an expert mechanic. There shouldn't be any problem having it towed and fixed."

Casbah. So the desert prince had an equally exotic lair. He probably had a harem of concubines too, she thought wryly. "I'd appreciate that." She turned and strode swiftly toward the black stallion. "Naturally I'll reimburse you for any expenses.

You've gone to enough trouble on my account already."

He was following more leisurely, his face lit with a smile of amusement. "No trouble, windflower. Pure pleasure, I assure you."

She turned to face him, frowning. "Look, you don't have to give me all that chivalrous guff," she told him impatiently. "I know you were only trying to make it easier for me by distracting me back at the hill. I don't expect you to keep it up now."

"That's very understanding of you," he said mildly as he placed his hands on her waist and lifted her into the saddle with easy strength. "If a trifle muddleheaded. I meant every single word, Billie."

"You couldn't possibly," she argued desperately as he swung up behind her. "It's completely insane. We're total strangers. I don't know anything about you." She ran her hand distractedly through her hair. "For heaven's sake, I don't even know your name, where you live, anything!"

He gathered up the reins, and the black started off at a trot. "I live in the Casbah in Zalandan in the sheikhdom of Sedikhan," he said calmly as his arm went around her waist in a protective embrace. "And my name is David Bradford."

Two

"It looks more like an ancient medieval fortress than a city." Billie's eyes were bright with curiosity as they took in the high stone walls that surrounded Zalandan, while they rode through an open wooden gate that was as tall as the walls themselves. "I half expect to see the caliph's guard thundering through the streets on horseback. Marasef was interesting, but this is really fascinating."

"I'm glad you approve." David's voice in her ear was amused. "But if you don't stop turning from side to side trying to see everything, you're going to fall off old Nick. It will all still be here tomorrow. I'll take you for a complete Cook's tour then. Now I want to get you home and arrange to send someone out to get your Jeep while there's light enough to see." His eyes gazed appraisingly at the slanting rays of the sun. "It should be sunset in an hour or so. That won't give anyone much time."

She leaned back against him with a resigned sigh. "Okay, tomorrow. But I want to see everything."

"Yes, ma'am," he drawled. "It will be as you command, *lallah*."

The cobbled square they crossed was utterly intriguing. It was lined with long rows of awning-covered stalls selling everything from leather goods, jewels, and exotic scents to Jaffa oranges and red-gold pomegranates. There were a number of alleyways leading off the bazaar. They turned off into one of them. The shadowed, winding street was crowded with whitewashed, flat-roofed houses and tiny shops, and Billie found the scene just as interesting as the marketplace.

And everywhere they went David was known and greeted. From the bazaar vendors to the little boy playing with his friends in the street he received warm smiles and was hailed with evidence of affection. Billie knew enough Arabic to get the gist of most of the salutations, but they addressed him with a word that was totally unfamiliar to her. She glanced over her shoulder at him, her brow knitted. "They're calling you 'Lisan.' What does that mean?"

To her amazement a dark flush mottled his cheeks. "It's a Sedikhan word," he said gruffly. "It's just a nickname they gave me when I first arrived in Zalandan." He lifted his arm, pointing, and said hurriedly, "The Casbah is just beyond that white stone wall."

If she'd thought Zalandan looked like a fortress, the Casbah was one in reality. The gate was guarded by two husky young men in the olive-green uniform of the Sedikhan army. They were standing at attention, their rifles slung over their shoulders with casual competence.

"Guns?" Billie asked bewilderedly. "And those uniforms are the real thing. I've seen soldiers in the streets of Marasef dressed like that. What kind of a place is this?"

They entered a huge flagstoned courtyard, and the building it fronted was more like a palace than a simple residence. Its arched windows and fretted balconies were like something from an Oriental dream. There was nothing dreamlike, though, about the two additional soldiers who stood on either side of the carved teak double doors of the front entrance.

"This is my home," David said soothingly. "You'll get used to the soldiers. They don't intrude at all, and you'll find they're very friendly once you get to know them. They only appear ferocious because Karim has them so intimidated. They're afraid even of smiling in case it's a breach of discipline."

"Karim? Who's Karim?"

"Karim is my friend. The Casbah belongs to him." David halted the stallion by a fountain and slipped blithely from the saddle. He tossed the reins to a grinning, white-clad boy who appeared out of nowhere. He lifted Billie down, and the boy led the horse away. "A very possessive fellow, Karim," he said lightly. "Sometimes I think he believes the whole world belongs to him."

"A good portion of it does," the heavyset man who emerged from the house said crisply. Dressed in dark jeans and a gray turtleneck sweater, his massive figure looked even more intimidating than the soldiers. He was somewhere in his fifties, his curly brown hair sprinkled lightly with gray and his rough craggy features creased in a frown. "And he's gobbling up more every day." His light blue eyes were definitely annoyed. "And you just may be next on the menu. Karim's been frothing at the mouth since he found out you went out again without a guard."

"He'll get over it," David said casually. "He knows I'm not going to submit to being trailed around like some comic-opera Ali Baba with his entourage. We've gone into all that before." He turned to Billie. "This irate gentleman is Clancy Donahue, Billie. He's head of Alex's security forces, but is on special assignment, trying to make my life miserable for the next few months. This is Billie Callahan, Clancy."

"Delighted," Donahue growled, barely glancing at her. "Better miserable than dead, David. Ladram is still out there somewhere, remember? If anything happened to you, I'd catch such hell from Alex and Sabrina, not to mention Karim, that I might as well resign from the human race."

"But nothing's going to happen to me," David said lightly. "I can take care of myself without a battery of bodyguards. You should know that better than anyone, Clancy. You're the one who taught me."

"Karate and judo aren't going to do you much good if Ladram decides to pick you off in an ambush."

"With a rifle?" David shook his head. "Ladram is a knife man. Every note he's sent me elaborates on the intense joy he's going to get from slicing off various portions of my anatomy. He's not going to give up that kick just to play it safe. A rifle would be too impersonal for him."

"Wait a minute." Billie held up her hand. "I know I'm supposed to be quietly ignoring the conversation like a good little guest, but you're driving me crazy. What the devil is going on? I feel like I've just stepped back onto a movie set." She shook her head. "No, that was more realistic than this. Guns and soldiers and knives. Why should your friend need a security force? Who are Alex and Sabrina? I think you should have left me back in that sandstorm. Everything was a lot clearer there."

"Sorry." David's smile was penitent. "We have been rude, haven't we, Billie? You have a perfect right to be confused. Let's see, what was the first question? Oh, the security force. Karim Ben Raschid still has a hell of a lot of enemies. A man who holds his position for almost fifty years doesn't necessarily shed them when he relinquishes his power. He officially gave up the sheikhdom to Alex four years ago, but he still wields an enormous amount of clout and can't resist dabbling occasionally."

"More than occasionally," Donahue snorted. "I think he's wheeling and dealing more now on the QT than he did when he was the reigning monarch of Sedikhan."

"Karim Ben Raschid," Billie repeated in bewilderment. "Your friend is the former ruler of Sedikhan? Then, Alex Ben Raschid, the present monarch, is his grandson. And Sabrina?"

"Is his wife," David said. His hand had propelled her up three shallow steps, and he was opening the front door. "An American, by the way. We grew up together on neighboring ranches in Texas. You'll like her, windflower. She's a very special lady. She's in Marasef at the moment, but I'll give her a call and see if she and Alex can fly out to meet you."

"You just give heads of state a ring and they drop

everything and come running?" Billie shook her head dazedly. "Who are you, David?"

"No one important, I'm afraid," David said, his eyes twinkling. "I'm a poor peasant in a nest of power figures. Naturally Alex and Bree will come only if it's convenient."

Donahue's snort was much more pronounced this time. "You know damn well they'll come if you ask them," he said gruffly. "The last time I talked to them on the phone, they were wondering when you were coming home."

"Zalandan isn't your home?" Billie asked.

David shrugged. "I usually divide my time between Marasef and here. You might say they're both my homes."

Her thoughts were whirling, but she suddenly remembered another bit of conversation. "Ladram. Who's Ladram?"

David's expression suddenly became guarded. "No one important. A very unpleasant fellow who's causing a little disturbance." He was pulling a red-and-gold-figured velvet bell and threw Donahue a warning glance as he started to protest. "You must feel as sand-logged as I do. I'm going to have you shown to your quarters so you can bathe and rest a little before dinner. I'll arrange to have your Jeep taken care of and have a little talk with Karim." He smiled warmly at the woman who appeared in answer to the bell. In her middle forties, she was very attractive in a serene and dignified way. Her dark hair was pulled back in a smooth chignon and her slightly plump form was garbed in a simple dark cotton gown. "This is Yasmin Dabala. Billie Callahan, Yasmin. She runs the Casbah and all its inhabitants with an iron hand, isn't that right, Yasmin?"

"One can only try," she answered tranquilly. "Sometimes foolish men rebel and disturb the patterns that are best for them." She frowned sternly. "Mr. Donahue said you went for your ride without a guard again. Very stupid, Lisan."

David made a face. "This is where I came in. Suppose you take Billie to her quarters and make her comfortable. That way I'll only have one of you to contend with." He gave Billie a little push in the housekeeper's direction. "Run along, sweetheart, you'll be safe with Yasmin. She never bites strangers, only her near and dear."

"That is true." Yasmin's reserved face softened, and her dark eyes lit with affection. "Only my near and dear, Lisan." She turned and started to glide gracefully down the polished mosaic-tile corridor. "If you will follow me, Miss Callahan?"

"Billie," she said as she hurried after her. She glanced over her shoulder to see David and Donahue still standing at the door watching her. Then she turned the corner and they were out of view.

"Very attractive," Clancy Donahue observed.

"I think so," David agreed, a little smile tugging at his lips. "But not at all sexy. She told me so."

Donahue's eyes narrowed. "Rather an intimate conversation for such a brief acquaintance. You just ran across her in the desert? Quite a coincidence running into an attractive American woman right outside your gates."

"I might have known your suspicious mind would latch on to that fact and start clicking away." David sighed ruefully. "I'll save you the trouble of interrogating her. She's only been in Sedikhan a few months, with the production company that's filming *Desert Venture* outside of

Marasef. Billie's an actress." Again that curiously tender smile curved his lips. "A lousy one, she tells me."

"She's obviously made quite an impression on you," Donahue said impassively. "She must be very charming."

"Charming?" David shook his head. "That's a little too conventional an adjective for Billie Callahan. She's part pixie and part wild thing."

"Sounds a bit uncomfortable." Donahue was gazing quizzically at the burnoose that David was shrugging out of. "Where the hell did you get that? You look like the male lead from *Desert Song*."

"Yasmin made it for me. I wear it occasionally so she'll know her gift has value for me," he answered as he draped the robe carelessly over his arm. "It came in handy in that sandstorm, though."

"Maybe that's why the bedouins made them *de rigueur*."

"Maybe," David said absently. "Look, Clancy, I want you to arrange things so Billie isn't permitted to leave Zalandan." At Clancy's startled glance he added quickly, "She's not to be hurt. Make sure of that. I just want her to stay at the Casbah."

"Then, you do think she has some connection with Ladram?" Clancy pounced swiftly.

"Ladram? Hell, no, you have that man on the brain." There was amused exasperation on David's face. "If I have the lady judged correctly, she really hasn't a connection with anyone on the face of the earth." He smiled. "But she's going to, Clancy. She's going to have an exceptionally intimate connection very soon." He shrugged. "But like I said, she's a very skittish, wild thing. I need a little insurance so I have the time to make that connection before she flies away."

"You'll get your insurance," Clancy said slowly, his expression thoughtful. "I think it would be a very good idea to detain Ms. Callahan for a while." He watched as David brushed futilely at his jeans, causing sand to cascade to the floor. "Why don't you go change before bearding Karim in his den? It looks like you brought half of the desert in with you. He's not going to be any more angry with you in fifteen minutes than he is now."

David shook his head. "I'll go right in to see him." He smiled gently. "Karim always roars loudest when he's worried. I'll just show him I'm all right and let him take the edge off his temper." He walked rapidly down the hall. "See you at dinner, Clancy."

Clancy gazed after him with an expression compounded equally of affection and exasperation. The assignment Alex had given him of protecting David was proving more difficult than if it were Karim himself he had to guard. David's gentleness covered a will that was even more inflexible than Alex's or that of the old tiger waiting for David in the study.

He could almost visualize David lounging in a chair in front of Karim's desk, listening patiently while the sheikh ranted and raved at him. There would be that same gentle smile on his face when Karim ran out of words and anger. He'd get up, say something soothing and noncommittal, and leave. He'd seen it happen a dozen times with Alex and Sabrina, and then it had only amused him. Now that he was the one being confronted by that iron determination, he wasn't quite so entertained. It wasn't bad enough having Ladram somewhere out there just waiting to pounce. Now there was Billie Callahan on the scene, who'd be an unknown element in an already explosive situation. And he could do without unknown elements appearing out of nowhere at this point. When David had finished with Karim, he'd be having a talk with the sheikh himself.

Billie's eyes widened with admiration as she was led down a long hall that contained a multitude of arches and tiny alcoves where Eastern carpets in rich, jewellike colors lay on gleaming mosaic tiles. Filigreed Moorish lamps hung here and there on long brass chains, softly lighting the magnificent paintings on the walls of the alcoves. The collection evidently included everything from the old masters to the most brilliant of the contemporary school. There was even a glowing island landscape by Rubinoff, she noted admiringly.

Yasmin opened the delicately carved cream-colored doors and preceded Billie into the suite. "I think you'll be comfortable here," she said. "The bathing chamber and dressing room are through there." She gestured toward an arched doorway hung with a diaphanous white net curtain. "Naturally, everything you require will be provided."

"Naturally." Billie wrinkled her nose impishly. "Where have you hidden Aladdin's lamp for me to rub?" She glanced blissfully at the wide ottoman bed hung with amber silken curtains, at the table inlaid with mother of pearl that stood beside the monster of a bed, then looked at the white filigree doors that must lead to her own private patio. "On second thought, I don't believe I need it. Glory, what a *sinfully* gorgeous room."

There was a trace of amusement in Yasmin's smile. "I am happy it pleases you, because I'm not certain, but I don't think we have Aladdin's lamp on hand."

"No matter," Billie said breezily. "The only thing I need now is a bath and a change of clothes. I won't even ask for minstrels or acrobats to keep me amused."

"I think we can fill your needs," Yasmin said. A frown suddenly darkened her face. "Though there may be difficulty finding a garment suitable for dinner." Her gaze went over Billie's slender figure, which had a fragility belied by the crackling vitality emanating from it. "You're quite slim, aren't you?"

"That's putting it kindly," Billie said glumly. "I've got less shape than Twiggy did in the 1960s." She gazed wistfully at Yasmin's full bodice. "No bazooms. Every woman in the world has great bazooms but me."

"Bazooms?" Yasmin's forehead wrinkled in puzzlement. "I don't know the word."

"Never mind. It's an American colloquialism," Billie told her. "You don't need me to mess up your English. It's quite beautiful. Where did you learn it?"

"I have been in Karim Ben Raschid's household since I was a child of ten," Yasmin said. "It was required that everyone entering his service learn English immediately and that we all attend school until we had at least the equivalent of your secondary education. Sheikh Ben Raschid would never tolerate ignorance around him."

"Ah, an enlightened monarch," Billie said. "Is it too much to hope he also believes in women's liberation?"

Yasmin's dark eyes danced. "Only on a general, not a personal, level," she answered demurely. "It is much, considering who he is." She turned away, moving with her unhurried grace. "If you'll be so kind as to run your own bath, I will see about finding you a dress that may be suitable."

"It will be a terrible strain, but I guess I can manage," Billie said lightly, already pulling the tunic over her head and receiving another shower of sand in the process.

Fifteen minutes later she was ensconced in a huge sunken tub tiled in an exotic cream-and-rose mosaic. She rinsed the last of the shampoo from her hair and leaned back against the tub enclosure. She shut her eyes and sighed in contentment. Lord, it felt wonderful to be clean again. It was odd that no matter what trouble one faced, the simple, primitive things in life always made the burden lighter. A bath, a hot meal, a warm fire, a bit of music.

Music. She felt a swift surge of pain as she remembered her shattered guitar. God, that had hurt. She hadn't been that upset about anything for a long, long time. It had been awfully dumb to let it get to her so much. After all, she wasn't a kid anymore. She'd felt like a child, though, and she'd welcomed David Bradford's understanding and warmth as if she were a heartbroken baby. His understanding hadn't completely healed the hurt, but it had helped. Great heavens, how it had helped.

How strange was the magic he could weave about her. She'd been off balance and on the defensive since the moment she'd encountered him. Why, when he was perhaps the least intimidating man she'd ever met? Why did he make her feel so threatened? Her reaction was as crazy as everything else connected with David Bradford.

It didn't really matter. She'd be gone from here in

another few days, and in a month he would be only a memory.

"Mr. Donahue has sent word he will be here to escort you to the library for cocktails in forty-five minutes." Billie opened her eyes to see Yasmin standing by the sunken tub, a large white bath sheet in her hands and a slight smile on her face. "Lisan has gone to the mechanic's quarters to see to the disposition of your automobile, but will be pleased to join you later for dinner. He has asked that I attend you personally rather than delegate a maid. Will that be satisfactory?"

Billie stood up and ascended the three marble steps, feeling a little embarrassed as she was wrapped gently in the sheet. "Look, I don't need anyone to 'attend' me. I wouldn't know what to do with a maid if I had one. All this Mideastern splendor is making me feel as if I'm being groomed for a harem girl. I'm sure you have something better to do than help me dress." She grinned mischievously. "I've been doing that just fine since I was three."

Yasmin cast a disparaging glance at the jeans and tunic Billie had tossed carelessly on the velvet stool of the vanity. "I'm sure you have, Miss Callahan," she said with polite determination. "But there's always room for improvement. Why don't you let me try?" She was pushing Billie through the diaphanous curtain into the main chamber. "I will make you beautiful for Lisan." Her eyes were narrowed as they ran critically over Billie's slim, towel-draped form. "You are very graceful." She tilted her head consideringly. "You aren't as womanly as the *kadines* Lisan usually favors, but he must find you to his taste. We will do what we can."

"Thank you," Billie said ironically. She'd been joking when she'd made that quip about being a candidate for a harem, but suddenly she felt exactly that way. She had found Yasmin very likable before, but now there was an element of steely obstinacy beneath that gentle courtesy. "I appreciate the fact that you're willing to make the effort, but you seem to have the wrong idea about Mr. Bradford and me. I'm just a temporary houseguest while my Jeep is being fixed. Nothing else. Understand?"

"If you say so," Yasmin answered serenely as she crossed to the bed and picked up a gleaming short dress of white lamé. "I think you'll find this dress adequate. It was left by one of Lisan's *kadines*. Miss Nazare was far more voluptuous, as I said, but this is a shift, and it will not matter too much. It is silk-lined, so the lack of undergarments will not be uncomfortable."

"Miss Nazare? Who is she?"

"No one important," Yasmin answered absently, still appraising the dress critically. "Just one of the *kadines* the shiekh flew in for Lisan's pleasure last month."

"*Kadine*? That's some glorified Mideastern call girl, isn't it?" Billie asked. Why was she feeling this sudden twinge of pain as she looked at the luscious scrap of lamé? What did it matter to her if Bradford had a hundred women to warm his bed? The man was nothing to her.

"You don't object to wearing such a woman's clothing?" Yasmin's brow knitted and her voice was earnest. "You must understand that in Sedikhan there is nothing degrading about the profession of *kadine*. These women choose their profession because it is a way to riches and even political power. It is a little like the Japanese gei-sha. Lisan would never use a woman unless she was willing and joyous in her giving. It is not his way."

"And does Karim Ben Raschid often import *kadines* for Mr. Bradford's pleasure?" She could have bitten her tongue. That was certainly none of her business, and she had absolutely no interest in the answer.

"Of course. Lisan is a very virile man, and the sheikh wishes him to be happy here at Zalandan." Her smile was indulgent as she removed the towel from Billie and slipped the dress over her head. "Sometimes I think Sheikh Karim and his grand-son act like small children competing for a favorite toy. They're both constantly trying to think up attractions that will keep Lisan with them." She shrugged. "But then, we're all like that about Lisan." She took a step back and smiled with satis-faction. "Yes, that is very lovely on you. You mustn't worry, he won't even remember who wore it last. Miss Nazare was nothing to him."

"I'm not worried," Billie said with exasperation. "I wouldn't care if his little *kadine* was the love of his life. He may be the fair-haired boy around here, but he's nothing but a chance acquaintance to me. Why won't you understand that?"

"Do not upset yourself." Yasmin's voice was soothing as she hustled Billie to an inlaid vanity and pushed her down gently on the amber-cushioned vanity bench. "If you feel nothing now, it will come. Soon you will be willing to give Lisan everything he wants from you."

"What he wants? Look, I told you we're practi-cally strangers. He's just playing the good Samari-tan. The only thing he's going to want from me is a thank you and a fare-thee-well." She could see by the passivity of the other woman's face that she just wasn't getting through. "I'm *not* one of his *kadines*!"

"I know that," Yasmin said composedly. "But Lisan wants you, and that is all that's important. He has a very special feeling for you or he wouldn't have asked me to care for you. He has never made such a request before." She picked up the portable hair dryer from the vanity. "Now, I will dry those pretty curls so that Lisan will look at you with pleasure." And the roar of the dryer cut Billie off in mid-protest.

The Sedikhan woman was obviously going to be as impossible to shift from her position as a tank, and Billie finally gave up the struggle and let her have her way. Thirty minutes later her copper hair was tumbling down her back in a cascade of stylishly careless curls, her features delicately accented with an artistry that would have done justice to an expert at Elizabeth Arden's. Billie gazed at her reflection in the mirror with a degree of surprise.

The white lamé shift was amazingly flattering on her. On its original owner it had probably been a subtle provocation, but on her own slight body it was like a delicate glittering icicle against the fiery vitality of her hair and the smooth, golden tan of her skin. Her bare shoulders looked positively alluring beneath the slender spaghetti straps. The dress reminded her vaguely of one of the flapper outfits of the roaring twenties. The matching high-heeled slides were a little big on her, but not too bad. David Bradford's *kadine* probably even had voluptuously beautiful feet, she thought crossly.

"It is fine," Yasmin said, spraying her lightly

with a scent that was hauntingly floral. "I would have done better if we'd had more time, but it will have to do. Mr. Donahue will be here in just a moment."

"I'm glad you're satisfied." Billie sighed. "I feel a little like a turkey that's been stuffed for Thanksgiving dinner."

"I have heard of your Thanksgiving turkey," Yasmin said with a smile. "Last year the sheikh had a complete authentic Thanksgiving dinner flown here from a fine hotel in New York as a surprise for Lisan. It made him very happy."

And, of course, that was the name of the game around here. It seemed that Yasmin's precious Lisan had only to lift a wistful eyebrow and everyone fell all over himself to give him whatever his heart desired. Well, she wasn't an expensive *kadine* or a Thanksgiving turkey, and she wasn't about to be gift-wrapped and presented to the golden prince of the desert.

Suddenly she chuckled as she realized she'd already been elaborately gift-wrapped, indeed, by the slavishly devoted Yasmin. It was all a little amusing, come to think of it, and there was no reason for her to come unglued about something so trivial.

"And I'm sure that fact sent the entire household into raptures," she said lightly. A discreet knock sounded, and she gestured for Yasmin to stay where she was. "I'll get it. I assume that's the grim Mr. Donahue, who will take me to the equally grim Sheikh Karim." She moved swiftly toward the door. "It's shaping up to be a really fun evening." She glanced over her shoulder as her hand closed on the knob of the door. "By the way, your Mr. Bradford said Lisan was a Sedikhan nickname. What does it mean?"

"A nickname?" Yasmin's smile was glowingly tender. "I suppose you might call it that," she said softly. "It means 'the beloved.' "

"You appear very thoughtful, Miss Callahan," Clancy Donahue observed as he altered his long-legged stride to match her shorter steps. They had crossed a bewildering maze of corridors in virtual silence, and now his cool blue eyes held a hint of curiosity.

"Do I?" Billie asked lightly, darting him a rueful glance. "Now, I wonder why I would have anything to think about? I've only been dropped into the middle of an armed fortress with security forces, royal heads of state, and mysterious allusions to death and mayhem. In addition, I have a feeling I've just been selected by Yasmin to honor the bed of an impossibly eccentric man who seems to be worshiped as some kind of god." She shook her head wonderingly. "Whoever heard of anyone's being called 'the beloved.' "

Donahue's hard face softened with a smile of amusement. "Yasmin told you about that? David's not going to be at all pleased. That little sobriquet embarrasses the hell out of him." The smile faded, and the keen eyes once more became guarded. "However, it's just as well you've been made aware of how everyone in Sedikhan feels about David. You're wrong about his being worshiped by the people here in Zalandan, but they do love him." His lips tightened. "And you can see David is protected by both Karim and Alex Ben Raschid, the two most powerful men in the Middle East. They're both very ruthless men, Miss Callahan, and David is very special in their eyes. Should I tell you what would happen to anyone who tried to harm him?"

Billie's eyes were wide with shock. The threat in Donahue's words had been too plain to be missed. "This is as absurd as all the rest," she said blankly. "For heaven's sake, are you actually suspecting me of being some kind of threat to your precious Lisan?"

"I'm a very suspicious man, Miss Callahan," Donahue answered quietly. "I'm especially suspicious of coincidences like the one that brought you and David together. You may not be a physical threat to David, though that's a distinct possibility. Actresses have been known to be hired to play Delilah before. Particularly second-rate actresses, as you confess to being." He shrugged. "Even if you're not in cahoots with Ladram, there's a chance you may be trying to hook a rich husband or protector. I assure you that Karim and Alex wouldn't like the idea of David's being used like that any more than they'd like him to be in physical danger."

"I don't even know the man," Billie sputtered, her violet eyes blazing. "I know nothing about him. How could I possibly know that David Bradford was wealthy?"

"A little investigation would have revealed that Karim transferred a few acres of property to David three years ago as a birthday present," he said cynically, "along with the fact that those acres are capable of yielding approximately the same amount of oil as the state of Oklahoma. It would also have made you aware that David was then in a state of near-mental retardation, a child in a man's body. He would have been ripe for any unscrupulous manipulation you might have had in mind."

Mental retardation. That golden man, with his wise, clear eyes? She felt a sickening pain somewhere deep inside. "No," she whispered. "You're lying. There's nothing wrong with David. There couldn't be."

Donahue's eyes were narrowed on her face. "You didn't know," he said slowly, and then a little smile lit the sternness of his face. "Unless you're a far better actress than you claim, I'd say you didn't have any prior knowledge of David's background."

"He's *not* retarded," Billie said desperately, feeling her throat tighten with tears. "He's intelligent, sharp, witty. He may be a little eccentric, but you can't tell me there's anything wrong with him mentally, dammit."

"Easy." For the first time there was a spark of warmth in the coolness of Donahue's eyes. "You're right, there's nothing wrong with David now. His mind is as keen as a scalpel, and as far as creativity goes, he's quite brilliant. I just said that three years ago he was still suffering from a . . . a state like mental retardation." His voice hardened. "While he was in college he experimented with one of the so-called mind-expansion drugs, and it damn near made a vegetable out of him. For years he was like a child, but gradually he began to regain the full powers of his mind. When Sabrina and Alex brought him to Sedikhan four and a half years ago, they weren't sure he'd ever be well again."

"But he did get well," Billie murmured, feeling a profound relief and thanksgiving that was as mysterious as all her other emotions in regard to David Bradford.

"Yes, he did get well," Donahue agreed. "I don't know if it was a natural recovery or the battery of doctors Karim commandeered from all over the world to treat him." There was a touch of amusement in his grin. "Karim had stepped down from his position as ruling head of Sedikhan, presumably for reasons of health. Actually, I think he just wanted to give Alex the experience of running the country while he was still hovering in the background. He needed something to focus his attention on, and he chose David. He whisked him away to Zalandan, using the excuse that Alex and Sabrina needed the time to get used to their new life at Marasef." Donahue chuckled reminiscently. "They didn't like it any too much, but tried to give in gracefully. Karim was an old man and had recently been very ill. Karim was all prepared to look upon David as a remote analytical problem to be solved and then returned to Sabrina and Alex. It didn't turn out that way, though."

"How did it turn out?"

"Karim learned to love David," Donahue said simply. "I don't think the old tiger had ever really loved anyone before in his life. He had a guarded affection for Alex and Alex's cousin, Lance, but they were both such strong, independent personalities that there was an element of competitiveness that kept him from giving that love totally. With David that barrier didn't exist. He was a beautiful, very special child who might remain that way for the rest of his life." His blue eyes twinkled. "Little did Karim know that once David recovered, he'd have another powerhouse to contend with. By that time it was too late. David had breached all the old man's defenses, and Karim was utterly devoted to him." Donahue's expression was suddenly thoughtful. "In spite of his regained mental powers, there's still a quality of childlike honesty and simplicity about him that's very moving. It arouses a fierce protectiveness in the people who care about him. If you do have any aims that might interfere with that protectiveness, you'd be wise to think twice, Miss Callahan."

"Are you back to that again?" Billie asked with a sigh. Somehow she was no longer feeling the anger she had before at Clancy Donahue's insinuations. There was something very likable beneath that grim facade. "I thought you'd come to believe that I knew nothing about David Bradford before I came to Zalandan."

"I want to believe you," he said soberly. "You're a very charismatic woman, and, I hope, an honest one. It's just my job to make sure of that, Miss Callahan."

"I suppose it is," Billie said with an impish smile. "It might be interesting, at that, to be regarded as some sort of *femme fatale*." She fluttered her long lashes vampishly at him. "Is this the way it's done? You'll have to excuse me, but I'm sinfully inexperienced in the role."

"I'm afraid it's very obvious," he said, his lips twitching. "Mata Hari you're not, Miss Callahan."

"Billie," she prompted as they paused before an intricately carved teak door. "It's ridiculous to be formal when we've already been through so much together. Anger, suspicion"—her voice lowered dramatically—"intrigue. And now you're evidently planning to play executioner." She gestured to the door. "The tiger's cage?"

"The tiger's cage," Donahue agreed with a grin. "But I have an idea you just might be able to handle him . . . Billie."

"Oh, I'll be able to handle him," she said breezily, reaching for the doorknob. "There's not much I can't handle, Clancy. Come along and watch my style."

Three

She stopped short just inside the door, her gaze on the portrait hanging on the wall over the desk.

"David," she whispered.

It was David and yet not David. The man kneeling with a trowel in his hand and the sunlight burnishing his hair to white gold was younger, more aesthetic-looking, less virile somehow. But beautiful. No one could argue that. He was in a garden, dressed in faded jeans and a worn blue work shirt. A blue-and-white bandanna was tied around his forehead as a sweatband, and his hair was pulled back into an odd shoulder-length braid, revealing the classic strength of his features. The braid and bandanna gave him a slightly savage aura, but there was nothing savage in the eyes gazing out of the portrait. Sapphire blue, clear and gentle, they were almost radiant with a strange wisdom and understanding. Yes, that was David.

"Exceptionally good, isn't it?" Clancy murmured into her ear.

"What?" she asked absently, then forced herself to look away from the portrait. "Oh, yes, remarkable." She shook her head as if to clear it and focused her attention on the man who was lolling lazily in the executive chair at the desk beneath that riveting picture.

A tiger, Donahue had called him, and Karim Ben Raschid looked every bit as ferocious as he rose lithely to his feet. The gesture appeared to be more a positioning for a lethal spring than a courtesy. Dressed in a flowing white burnoose open down the front to reveal an impeccable black tuxedo, Karim had the powerful, vigorous body of a man of forty. There was only a dusting of gray in his dark hair and beard, and his flashing dark eyes were as piercing and dangerous as a hawk who'd sighted prey. Only his strong, gnarled hand toying with a gold pen indicated the years that he carried so lightly.

"Ah, Miss Callahan, welcome to my home." His voice was as smooth and mellow as a cello, and his smile wholly charming. "David and Clancy told me how lovely you were, but they weren't eloquent enough. What a beautiful treasure you are to ornament my Casbah."

Oh, Lord, she really wasn't up to all this flowery bull after her recent confrontation with Clancy. If she was going to be forced to stay here for the next few days, she'd better try to clear the air right away. Her feet sank into the pile of the rich Kirman carpet as she marched across the room to stand before the desk.

"Sheikh Ben Raschid, I'm grateful for your hospitality, and I know I'm supposed to answer you with a phrase that's as fancy and phony as yours." She drew a deep breath and raised her chin belligerently. "I want you to know that I realize what I'm *supposed* to do. I have no intention of doing it."

There was a flicker in Ben Raschid's dark eyes. "Indeed?" he said slowly. "And just what do you intend to do, Miss Callahan? I gather courtesy isn't high on your list of priorities."

"Courtesy rates very high, but hypocrisy comes in below zero," she said meeting his eyes steadily. "I found out a long time ago that I couldn't live like that. So what do you say we put our cards on the table? Clancy, here, seems to think I may be involved in some sort of plot to either snag the apple of your eye or massacre him. Will you believe me when I say I have no intention of doing either? That three days from now you'll have seen the last of me? I'd never even heard of this Ladram fellow before today."

"Your candid approach is very convincing, Miss Callahan," Ben Raschid said coldly. "I, too, have a dislike for hypocrisy, though I find it valuable upon occasion. It occurs to me you could have been coached to appeal to that preference."

"Oh, for heaven's sake, just look at me." Billie threw her arms out in frustration. "What kind of nutty villain would choose a lure like me? I'm not even sexy. I have my moments, but I'm definitely not the material *kadines* are made of."

"Yet you evidently exert a certain fascination for David," Ben Raschid answered. "He was quite insistent that I welcome you with all cordiality. Perhaps Ladram is more clever than we'd supposed. I didn't think he had that degree of subtlety, but hatred can bring out the cunning in rats like Ladram." His eyes narrowed. "He's on the run, so it wouldn't be possible for him to pay you exorbitantly. I, on the other hand, have unlimited resources. If you care to switch sides and confide Ladram's whereabouts, I'm prepared to be very generous." His smile was so lethal, she shivered involuntarily. "When Ladram is captured, his treatment is going to be most painful, and ultimately fatal. You wouldn't want to share in that fate, I assure you."

Good heavens, the man was a barbarian. "You sound quite savage," she said lightly, trying to smile. "What did the poor man do to arouse such a thirst for vengeance?"

"That 'poor' man was one of the kingpins of vice and narcotics in Sedikhan," Clancy said dryly as he strolled forward to stand beside her. "He was also rumored to have connections with the Mafia, but they seem to have deserted him. They didn't like the kind of heat David generated when he broke up the ring and sent Ladram on the run. That was eight months ago, and Ladram's been bombarding David with threatening letters and phone calls ever since."

"Knives," she whispered, remembering David's flippant words.

"How did you know that?" Ben Raschid asked in a harsh, guttural tone.

"David mentioned it," Clancy interjected swiftly. "I was there."

"So quick to the defense, Clancy?" Ben Raschid's voice was silky soft. "I think perhaps she may be even more clever than I thought."

"And now I'm supposed to have vamped your trusty right hand from his duty? How can I convince you that I'm just not that appealing?"

"You can't, Billie," David said softly from the

door. "Anyone would have to be blind not to see how sweet you are." He strolled forward. His golden good looks were set off beautifully by the elegant black tuxedo he was wearing, and his brilliant blue eyes were twinkling. "None of us are immune."

"Bull," Billie said succinctly. "Will you stop that? I'm having a rough time as it is trying to convince everyone I'm not after your scalp, either figuratively or literally."

"Not exactly seductive, Karim," Clancy murmured, his lips quirking.

Ben Raschid shrugged. "But challenging and a little intriguing, which could accomplish the same end with a man like David."

"You see? Everything I do is wrong. They're determined to view me as Lucrezia Borgia incarnate."

"Poor baby." David's face was alight with amusement. "They are giving you a hard time, aren't they? You're holding up better than most, though." His smile faded as he glanced at Karim, and his tone cooled considerably. "Testing her mettle, Karim? I asked you to make her welcome, not to intimidate her."

To Billie's amazement Karim actually looked disconcerted. "I tried to play the civilized host," he growled defensively. "She wouldn't let me. It seems the lady has a dislike for the social graces. She practically attacked me."

"Interesting." David's eyes were dancing as they went from Billie's indignant face to Karim's ferocious scowl. "You appear to have survived her assault very well, and perhaps it's just as well the amenities were dispensed with in the first confrontation." He smiled at Billie with a glowing intimacy. "I'm glad you have no use for games. Neither do I, windflower. It's going to escalate the pace of our relationship immensely."

"We have no relationship," she said, running her hand abstractedly through her hair. "That's what I've been trying to tell everyone. What I've been trying to tell *you*." She glared up at him. "And I do think you like to play games. I think it's amusing you to make some kind of play for me to while away a day or so in your little desert Shangri-La. I don't think you care a snap of your fingers what I think or feel."

David sobered instantly. "You're wrong, Billie," he said quietly. "They really have upset you, haven't they?" He took her hand in his. "I won't have that. We don't have time to waste with anger and hurt feelings. I want you to be able to concentrate on forming new emotional responses." He turned to Karim and said tersely, "I think we'll dispense with any type of formal dinner. I'm taking Billie with me to my suite. We'll dine there and perhaps I can repair some of the damage you've done. The next time you see her, I hope you'll take the opportunity to apologize.

Karim flushed. "Apologize! She's no delicate shrinking violet. She's a very tough lady. I think she came through the encounter better than I did."

"She's strong, but she's sensitive enough underneath all that brashness to be hurt," David said as he turned and pulled her toward the door. "I won't have her hurt, Karim."

"David—"

David turned, and when he saw the pleading that warred with the pride in Karim's fierce hawk eyes, he smiled very gently. "It's all right, Karim. It's just that you've made a mistake. She's special to me, and you must treat her with kindness. It's very important to me."

"It's you who are making a mistake," Karim said heavily. "It's dangerous to trust her. Even more since she is strong. You respond to strength, David. Weakness in others arouses your sympathy, but strength attracts you. Ladram would know that. He's made a study of you."

"It's not a mistake," David said softly. "Can't you see she wouldn't use that strength to do anything but help?"

"No, I can't see that." Karim's voice was roughly impatient. "And neither can you. She's an unknown quantity."

"I know her very well." David's smile encompassed her in a sunrise of warmth. "And I'm going to know her even better. Get used to the idea, Karim." The door closed behind them, shutting out the sight of Karim's frowning face and Donahue's smile of amusement.

Then David's hand was beneath her elbow and he was hurrying her through the mosaic corridors at a pace that had her half skipping to keep up with him. "Sorry about that, Billie. I should have realized they would react like that and been there to support you. It won't happen again. Karim knows I'm dead serious now."

"That's more than I do," Billie said wryly. "I can't believe any of this is really happening. Would it be too much to ask you to slow down so I can catch my breath?"

"Literally or figuratively?" His pace slowed as he glanced down at her. "Both, I think," he decided. "I'm moving too fast for you, aren't I, windflower? You need time to catch up and grow into your own knowledge of me." His eyes were grave. "I promised you that time, and I won't go back on it. I won't force that growth."

"Why should you, when everyone else is willing to do it for you?" Billie grumbled. "Yasmin almost served me up on a silver platter." She touched the glittering lamé dress. "She informed me that there wasn't much she could do to make me as glamorous as your last *kadine*, but this was her best effort."

"Is that who it belonged to?" David asked, his gaze running over her admiringly. Again she had that sensation of warm sunlight flowing over her. "I thought it was vaguely familiar. It looks different on you, sweetheart."

"I imagine it does," Billie said dryly. "According to Yasmin, Miss Nazare was considerably more voluptuous."

"That's not what I meant," David said. "On Shareen, it was just a dress. On you it's like a precious shimmering vase to hold my bright, glowing flower-girl." His eyes were twinkling. "And for your information, I'm finding you much more provocative in it than I ever did Shareen."

"That's difficult to believe," Billie said a trifle breathlessly, looking away from him.

"I know." David sighed, shaking his head. "You're not sexy, right? I can see something's got to be done to set you straight on that score." The amusement suddenly vanished. "Does the thought of Shareen bother you? It shouldn't, Billie. I'm no saint. I need sex, like any other man, but that was all it was with Shareen and the others." His voice was warm and deep. "I took pleasure and I tried to give it back, but what happens between us is going to be entirely different."

"Oh, Yasmin assured me she was nothing to

you," Billie said lightly, trying to keep the warmth he was exuding from flooding her being.

David frowned. "That wasn't true. Everyone has value and gifts to give. I'd be an unappreciative bastard to denigrate the giver of those gifts." His hand tightened on hers. "It's just that some gifts have more value than others. Physical satisfaction can mean a hell of a lot. But joy"—his deep blue eyes were glowing softly—"joy can last forever, Billie."

She forgot to breathe, and felt that dizzying warmth move languidly through her veins. Why was she letting him do this to her? She'd always moved so lightly on the surface of life, pausing to touch and enjoy relationships and adventures and then moving on. None of it had really affected her, but she knew with a little thrill of panic that if she let herself stay in this small circle of sunlight, she might never want to move on again.

"No!" She jerked her hand away from his and nervously smoothed the sleek material of the dress over her hips. "All this has nothing to do with me. Why can't you understand that?" She smiled with an effort. "And you say everyone is valuable and has gifts to give. What about this Ladram I've been hearing about? He doesn't seem to have much to give to the human race."

For the first time since she had met him, his face hardened and the warmth entirely left his eyes. "I stand corrected," he said curtly. "In every garden there are weeds that try to smother and destroy the useful and beautiful around them." His smile had the cold glitter of a stiletto. "The only thing you can do to prevent their doing that is to pluck them out and destroy them first."

She shivered as if the sun had suddenly gone

behind a cloud. She'd wanted to distract him and change the conversation, but this facet of David's character frightened her a little. "Another flower allusion," she said. "Your conversation certainly abounds with them. I suppose it's natural, considering you're something of a gardener. I saw that picture of you in the study. Was it painted here in Zalandan?"

He shook his head, his expression softening. "Lance Rubinoff painted that in the garden of the palace at Marasef. I have a garden here, too, but I think I like the one in Marasef better. It's outdoors, and I've always liked the sun on my face and the wind in my hair. The air is too dry and harsh, here in the middle of the desert, for plant life to flourish, so Karim built me a greenhouse to work in. It's very special to me too." His face was grave. "I want to share it with you, but not right now, Billie. I want to save it for a time that will be special to us both. Now we're just beginning to push through the earth to see the sun. I want to save it for the blossoming. Okay?"

The blossoming. What a beautiful and moving phrase. Almost as beautiful as the honey darkness of his voice when he said the words. "Okay," she said dreamily, and was rewarded by that sudden blinding smile.

"Good." He'd stopped before a carved teak door much like the one that graced the library, and he threw it open with a little flourish. "Now, step into my chamber and we'll talk of shoes and ships and sealing wax, of cabbages and kings." He winked. "And if you're extremely lucky, I might just let you bolt down a morsel or two of food in between."

David's suite was even more luxurious and lovely than her own, if a trifle more masculine. The white mosiac floor was covered with a cream-and-beige Aubusson carpet, and the coverlet on the wide ottoman bed was the flaming scarlet of autumn leaves. One wall was dominated by a huge, age-silkened rosewood desk, where an IBM Selectric typewriter, several piles of paper, and a stack of books offered a surprisingly workmanlike contrast to the antique desk. There were plants and greenery everywhere, and one particularly lovely plant with exquisite white blooms stood tall and proud in a glossy ebony planter in the corner.

"Sit down." David gestured to a scarlet-cushioned cane chair. He was shrugging out of his tuxedo jacket as he strode swiftly across the room toward another carved door. "I'll be with you in just a minute. I'll order our dinner to be served here and get rid of all this sartorial glory." He grimaced. "Karim likes us to dress for dinner, but it's all a little too grand for a cowboy like me."

Billie gazed musingly at the intricate carving on the door even after it had closed behind him. Gardener, cowboy, friend of sheikhs and princes, Lisan. He was so many things, and wherever she turned a new facet was revealed. What would she discover next? Her gaze was drawn irresistibly toward those curiously workmanlike stacks of papers beside the typewriter and she found herself pulled across the room as if to a magnet.

Manuscript pages, very professional, with "Bradford" and the page number neatly typed in the upper right-hand corner. Her lips curved in tender amusement. Another facet revealed. It appeared that David was an aspiring author. Then her smile faded as something tugged at her memory, and she reached slowly for one of the two leather-bound volumes that sat carelessly on the corner of the desk. It was lettered in gold, and she knew even before she saw the spine what the script would say. She had a well-thumbed paperback copy in her duffel in the jeep. *The Growing Season*, by David Bradford, an incredibly moving novel that had sent critics into ecstasies and was still on the best-seller list after nine months.

"I'd like you to read it when you get the time," David said quietly from the doorway. "A lot of me went into that book. I think you might get to know me a bit faster through it." He was dressed in dark cords and was rolling up the sleeves of a soft cream shirt, which was left open to reveal the bronze column of his throat.

"I already have," Billie said huskily. "It's the most beautiful book I've ever read." She laughed shakily. "But you don't need me to tell you that. The critics are calling it the book of the century, a classic. I've been haunting the bookstores for your second one."

"It came out four weeks ago," David said carelessly. "My publisher says it's doing better than the first one."

"That's understandable." Her fingers moved caressingly over the smooth leather spine. "Everyone wants to touch something special, even if it's only for a moment." Her eyes lifted to meet his across the room. "You spoke of giving gifts. I'd like to thank you for giving me this one. It could have been written for me personally." She shrugged and tried to laugh. "I'm sure millions of people feel the same way. That's probably why it's going to be a classic."

"I don't know about that," David said, making a face. "I had no idea everybody would make such a fuss about it when I submitted it. I just wanted to

tell a story and try to create something beautiful."
His expression became thoughtful. "I was restless
and searching for something to do with my mind
that would give me the same satisfaction I received
from working with my plants." There was a flicker
of excitement in the depths of his eyes. "I found
almost more than I had bargained for when I
started to write. It's like planting a brand-new garden with each story—plotting, then developing the
characters, then nurturing and watching the story
grow and blossom in your mind and then on the
paper before you." He shook his head and smiled
apologetically. "Sorry, it's all still new to me. I'm a
little overenthusiastic." He closed the distance
between them, took the book out of her hand and
tossed it casually on the desk. "My editor sent me a
copy of my second book. If you'll accept it, I'd like to
give it to you."

"No, I couldn't. . . ." she started politely. Then
she bit her lip as she saw the flicker of hurt in his
eyes. To hell with convention. That glimmer of
pain had started an aching somewhere near her
heart, and she *wanted* that book. It would be
almost like having a part of this beautiful, eccentric boy-man with her always. "Yes," she said
impulsively. "Yes, please."

A brilliant smile lit his face. "I'll send it to your
suite tomorrow. Tonight I want you to concentrate
on the man, not the author." There was a soft
knock on the door. "But first I'll let you concentrate
on dinner. Karim has an excellent chef. Let's see
what he has for us."

Throughout the meal that followed she was only
vaguely conscious of the exotic dishes set before
her by the deft, white-clad servant. Her attention
was centered solely on the golden man seated

across the small, damask-covered table. The conversation was light, the silences wonderfully comfortable, and always she was conscious of that magical pool of sunlit warmth that surrounded her. It melted all restraint, and she found herself deliberately blacking out everything but this moment. Why shouldn't she enjoy herself for the short time she was here? It had been ridiculous to be so wary and afraid of the responses David was arousing within her. She always welcomed new experiences, and this promised to be one of the most exciting yet. She felt a little tingle of excitement as she realized what that experience might entail. She found anticipation growing steadily as the servant cleared the table and filled the fluted crystal glasses with a clear golden wine that was no more heady than the thought of what might be.

She'd been aware of David's gaze on her face for the last ten minutes, and the expression in his eyes was a combination of amusement, tenderness, and the same excitement that was surging through her. Such beautiful eyes, so warm and loving and wise.

The door had scarcely closed behind the servant when David decisively set his glass down on the table. "I thought he'd never leave," he said with a boyish grin. He pushed back his chair, stood up, and was around the table in seconds. He took her glass from her hand and set it on the table before pulling her to her feet. "Come on, windflower, let's see if we can push those slips a little higher into the sun."

"Where are we going?" she asked, startled.

"I want to touch you," he said simply. "And I think you want to touch me, too, don't you, sweetheart?" He was leading her toward the wide, scarlet-draped bed. "I'm not going to force the pace, but I don't see why we can't have a little of what we want now." He stopped beside the bed and met her eyes gravely. "Unless I've read you wrong?"

He was giving her the chance to back away. To pretend and play games if that was what she wanted. That wasn't what she wanted. She'd always hated games, and, facing those clear, honest eyes, she knew she'd never be able to play them with David. "You haven't read me wrong," she said shakily. "It's crazy, isn't it? We only met this afternoon." She licked her lips nervously. "I've never done anything like this before."

"Haven't you?" David pushed her gently down on the bed and sat down beside her. "There's nothing to be nervous about. It's all perfectly natural and beautiful. Like I said, we're only going to caress the petals and breathe in the scents. You already know a little about my body, as I know about yours." His eyes twinkled. "We're just going to enlarge that knowledge without having a sandstorm to distract us." He slowly eased a narrow strap down from her shoulder, and the very deliberateness of the motion caused a little tingle of heat to go through her. "Such pretty shoulders. They look so fragile and fine-boned, but they're not really." His head bent, and his lips brushed the soft hollow beneath her collarbone. "They're strong and sturdy, just like the rest of you." He pushed her gently back in a reclining position on the bed and smiled down at her while he slipped the other strap from her shoulder. "I'm glad you're so strong and healthy, love. It would worry me to death if you were frail."

"I've always been strong as an ox," she said breathlessly, and closed her eyes in disgust. "Oh,

Lord, that sounded romantic as hell. I told you I wasn't used to situations like this."

She heard his low chuckle and then felt the shock of his lips on her other shoulder. "You're doing fine," he drawled, and she felt herself shifted as he lay down beside her. "And soon you'll be doing even better."

"You would have a red bedspread," she chattered nervously. "I look terrible in red. My hair . . ." She inhaled sharply as she felt the silken warmth of his lips on the rise of her breast. Her lashes flew open to see the sun-lightened gold of his hair only a few inches away. "It clashes," she whispered.

"I didn't notice," he said as he lifted his head to look down at her. He brushed a copper curl behind her ear. "So it does." His eyes held hers as he slowly bent so that his lips were hovering tantalizingly over her own. "But we don't clash, do we, love? We fit together." He was brushing her with quick, gentle kisses between every phrase. "We complement each other. Your softness against my hardness." He rubbed the slight stubble of his cheek against her with sensuous pleasure. "Your smoothness against my roughness." He placed his hand lightly on her throat, observing with pleasure the bronze darkness of his skin against her lighter, creamy gold. "Even the colors are right." His lips dipped to cover her own in a kiss of such exquisite tenderness that it made her throat ache with emotion. "All of our togetherness is right." He kissed her again. "And it always will be. Forever, Billie."

Her hands moved up to curl in the thick crispness of the hair at the nape of his neck. Forever. It sounded so beautiful, she thought, as beautiful as this dreamlike loving. Suddenly she stiffened and pushed him a little away. This wasn't a dream, and she didn't believe in forever. Not for her. She couldn't let this weaver of magic be fooled into thinking she did. He was already too dear to her to risk hurting. "No," she said quietly, her hands moving with unconscious yearning over his shoulders. "Now. Tomorrow. Perhaps the next day. But not forever, David. You've got to know that."

His eyes narrowed on her troubled face. "Poor little windflower. You're trying your best not to hurt me, aren't you? That conscience of yours won't let you take your pleasure without being sure that no one is going to suffer for it." He took her hands from his shoulders and held her palms against his chest. "Don't worry. You've given me fair warning. I'm not going to blame you if I come out of this with a scar or two." He was moving her hands up and down over the strong, supple muscles of his chest, an expression of almost feline pleasure on his face. "Some things are worth risking a great deal for." Then, as she opened her lips to speak, he dipped his head and sealed them with a long kiss that took her breath away and caused her lips to part yearningly to have more of him.

She could feel his heart begin to thunder beneath her palms as he began to taste with the delicate hunger of a gourmet who wished to savor every nuance of an exquisite feast. He explored the smoothness of her teeth, the warm darkness of her mouth, before stroking her tongue with an erotically teasing finesse that caused an aching heat to begin to build between her thighs. He raised his head, his chest laboring with the force of his breathing, a pulse leaping erratically in the hollow of his throat. "Turnabout is fair play, love," he said hoarsely. "Would you like to taste me too?" She nodded slowly, her gaze fixed compulsively on the parted lips so close to her own. "Then, come to me. Take me."

She needed no second invitation. She pulled his head down with a trembling eagerness, her tongue exploring his lips and teeth with delight before capturing his tongue with her lips and sucking gently. He stiffened and groaned deep in his throat, his hips suddenly jerking forward against the cradle of her thighs. He plunged his tongue deeper within her, pressing the hollow of her cheeks gently with his fingertips, and she obeyed the signal by increasing the pressure and nibbling teasingly with her teeth. He jerked again, and she could feel his heart trying to burst through the wall of his chest. He raised his head and drew a deep, shaky breath, his eyes dark and glazed. "We'd better stop that, sweetheart. It comes too close to the real thing. I keep thinking of how sweet and hot it's going to be when I'm drawn into you and held that tightly." He moved down and rested his head lightly on her breast. "Your heart is beating as crazily as mine." He rubbed his head back and forth against her. "And it's causing mine to beat even harder to know I can make you that excited." His hands were at the top of her dress. "I want to feel your heart under my hand. I want to taste your pretty breasts. Is that all right with you, windflower?"

"You'll be disappointed," she said shakily. "I'm not exactly voluptuous."

"I won't be disappointed." He was pushing the dress carefully down to her waist, his eyes burningly intent on her small naked breasts. "Lovely," he said softly. "Round, firm, and perfectly shaped, like creamy tulips with delicate pink centers." His hand cupped her gently, his probing fingertips engendering a throbbing that spiraled in intensity. "I want to feel you respond as I suck the nectar from those pretty flowers," he said thickly, lowering his lips to her nipples, which were already budding in invitation. His fingertips pressed over her heart with a light testing pressure as his lips closed on her. He gave a low growl of primitive satisfaction as her heart jumped wildly when he began the tender pulling suction that sent a rioting flame to the center of her being. The thumb and forefinger of his other hand began to roll the taut crest of her other breast, alternating gentle and rough pressure in tempo with the suckling of his mouth and tongue.

She cried out and arched up against him, her hips searching blindly. "You like that?" he muttered, his teeth nipping gently at her. "Oh, God, so do I. I love to touch you. I wish I could have you like this always. Naked and swollen and just waiting for my hand and lips. I don't see how I'm going to get through the next few days without taking you." His warm tongue brushed the other tip held between his fingers. "I'm going to need something to hold me. Don't put anything on between us. Okay? I want to know there's just you, sweet and warm and clean beneath your clothes. And when I can't take it any more, I want to be able to unbutton those clothes and take these pretty things out and hold them. Will you let me do that, Billie?"

"Yes, if you like," she murmured, her face flushed and languid. She would have promised him anything at that moment. She felt as if she were melting inside, liquid and flowing with emotions that were burning her with a blue-white flame.

"I like." The creases at the corners of his eyes deepened as he suddenly grinned. "And that's a hell of an understatement, love." His hands left her as he sat up and rapidly unbuttoned his shirt. "And now I'd like to feel all that soft roundness against me. Will you oblige me there, too, Billie?"

He didn't wait for a reply, but jerked open the cream shirt. The triangle of hair on his chest was a deeper gold, almost tawny, and looked invitingly soft and springy. "Sit up," he urged, his arms going around her to pull her up into his arms. The scent of spice and musk wafted around her as she buried her face in the soft, downy pelt. Then he was pressing the center of her back, arching her to meet warmth with warmth, softness with smoothness. So alike, yet so different. She could feel herself swell and burn as he rubbed against her like a sleek, sinuous cat. "When I'm inside you, I'm going to do this," he said, closing his eyes and holding her very still against him. "I'm going to lean over and love you with every inch of me. Can you see it, Billie?"

She could see it so well, it stopped her breath. "Yes," she said haltingly. It was hard to speak over the lump in her throat. She was so charged with emotion, she didn't know whether it was passion or something else that caused that odd poignant ache. "I can see it, David."

He was curiously taut and stiff for a long moment, and then she felt him make a conscious effort to relax his rigid muscles. He pushed her away from him, and his lids flicked open. His eyes were no longer glazed, but brilliant and warm. So warm. He kissed her gently on the forehead.

"Then, keep on seeing it, Billie." His hands were pulling up the bodice of her dress and slipping the slender straps over her shoulders. "See it. Hold it. Remember it. Until the blossoming."

"Until the blossoming," she repeated softly. There was a wrenching ache deep inside her, and she knew David was probably hurting with a frustration as intense as her own. Yet she wasn't even tempted to try to alter his decision to wait for the growth that would fulfill the promise of what they'd known tonight. She was filled with a strange glowing serenity like nothing she'd ever known before. She pulled away from him and began to button his shirt while he watched her with that tender half smile.

"You're still trembling," he said quietly. He touched her cheek lightly with a forefinger. "But then, so am I. It was beautiful, wasn't it, windflower?"

"Yes, it was beautiful," she said softly, meeting his eyes steadily. "Very beautiful." She tried to smile. "And now I think I'd better leave you and say good night."

He frowned and obviously was about to protest. Then he nodded slowly. "You're right." He stood up and pulled her to her feet. "I'd better get you out of here right away. I just didn't want to let you go." He slipped his arm around her waist with a casual familiarity that was both affectionate and endearing, as he accompanied her to the door. "I'll walk you to your suite."

She shook her head as she opened the door and turned to face him. "I'd rather be on my own. I've got to find my way around this labyrinth sometime. It might as well be now."

He nodded wryly. "I think you'll always be able to

find your way, Billie. I don't want to lead you or follow you. I just want to walk beside you." He
touched the tip of her nose gently, with a teasing
finger. "But I can wait. Be as independent as it
pleases you to be tonight. I'll pick you up tomorrow
morning at about eight and we'll have breakfast in
the bazaar before I take you on that sight-seeing
tour I promised you." He gave her another warm
smile before gently closing the door.

She turned and walked slowly down the corridor,
a tiny frown knitting her forehead as she realized
the forlornness she was feeling was born of an
emotion she'd never before let herself experience.
How odd after all these solitary years at last to
know loneliness.

Four

"Are we to be so honored as to see the treasures you've gathered in the back of your shop, Hassan?" David asked with solemn formality, gazing down at the eggshell fragility of the demitasse cup full of mint tea that he held. "I have heard wonderful stories of the Kirmans and Harizs you save for the eyes of only the chosen few."

Billie choked and tried to mask her giggle with a dignified cough, carefully keeping her gaze on her own cup. Oh, heavens, here we go again. She'd no idea David had such an impish sense of humor, until this afternoon.

"Certainly, Lisan, it is my pleasure," Hassan answered eagerly. "Naturally I was planning on showing you nothing but the best of my humble merchandise." He set his own cup down on the elaborately carved tray, uncrossed his legs, and rose from the cushions to his feet. "If you will follow me, I will show you carpets that will dazzle your eyes." He bustled toward a rich paisley wall hanging.

"Another back room?" Billie murmured, setting her cup down on the tray.

"Why not?" David asked blandly. "Everyone knows that all the real quality stuff is always kept away from the crude gaze of the hoi polloi." He stood up, looking down at her with a mischievous grin. "You did want to go on a real Mideastern shopping trip, remember?"

"I was just thinking of browsing in the bazaar again."

"Uh-uh." David shook his head as he took her hand and pulled her up from the enormous cushion. "We did that yesterday. You nearly walked my legs off, and the day before that we had to go sightseeing." He grimaced. "Hell, I never knew a small city like Zalandan could have so many sights. You must have found every historic site and tourist trap since the town was founded."

"I told you I wanted to see everything," Billie said with a grin. "What's the use of visiting a place unless you can capture a little of the flavor and atmosphere?" She wrinkled her nose teasingly at him. "Besides, I've never been escorted around a city by someone who had the honorary key to it. All doors are opened to Lisan. They even overlook your peculiar preference for ladies who wear jeans and look more like boys than women."

"That's not all that peculiar here in the Mideast," David said, sapphire eyes twinkling. "And I thought I'd convinced you that you definitely have no resemblance to a boy, windflower. I think it's about time we headed for that back room. You need another lesson."

"Again?" Billie's lips were twitching. "This is the

third one we've been in this afternoon. First there was the perfumery." She sniffed delicately at the sleeve of his blue, oxford-cloth shirt. "You still smell a little of lilacs. Then there was the coppersmith . . ."

"That was a mistake," David admitted. He slipped an arm around her waist and propelled her toward the hanging where the obsequiously smiling Hassan was waiting. "How did I know there'd be all those copper pots and cooking utensils hanging from the ceiling? I was the one who nearly knocked myself out. After that, I figured that a carpet shop would be just what the doctor ordered." He pushed her gently through the arched doorway and answered Hassan's low salaam with a polite one of his own. Then the paisley hanging slid gracefully into place. "Alone at last." He whirled and pushed her down on the pile of exotic carpets in the center of the room. "Now, *this* is what I call an interesting shopping trip."

The tiny room was dusky, and the rich carpets hanging on the walls gave off an aura of timeless intimacy. Billie was choking with laughter as she gazed up at him. His blue eyes were dancing, and a lock of sun-burnished hair was hanging rakishly over his forehead. He looked so like a little boy who had put some deviltry over on the grownups that she experienced a sensation of melting tenderness. "It's certainly a different one, anyway. Are we actually going to look at the merchandise this time?"

"Of course." David dropped down beside her on the bed of carpets, took her in his arms, and bore her back on the cushioned softness. "I intend to examine them very carefully." He ran his fingers through her hair before he spread the copper curls out on the cream-and-spring-green pattern of the carpet. "See what careful attention I'm paying to the colors and textures of the weave?" He rolled her over so that she was facing him. "How I'm testing the resilience of the pile?" His hands were on the front of her shirt, rapidly unbuttoning it. "Now there's only the final examination of softness."

Her eyes widened as they flew to the paisley hanging. "David, I don't think—"

"I told you it was considered bad manners to disturb a buyer while he was examining the merchandise," David said soothingly. "Hassan would cut off his arm rather than barge in here." He shook his head ruefully. "If you recall, old Said didn't even come to the rescue when I ran into the copper samovar and yelled like a banshee." He had her shirt open, and his hands were cupping and fondling her affectionately. "Sweet, so sweet."

It was sweet, she thought, gazing dreamily at his tanned, skillful hands on her paler flesh. For the moment there was nothing particularly sexual in the caress. In the past three days she'd found David was one of the most tactile persons she'd ever met. She'd remembered what he'd said about liking the wind and sun on his face while he was gardening. She could understand that now, after being the object of that sensual tactility. He was constantly touching her hair, playing with her fingers, running his hand in a long caress down her thigh, whenever they had a moment of privacy. In another man it might have been an annoying imposition, but this wasn't the case with David. It was all done with such loving affection and simple delight that it made her feel like a precious treasure being polished and caressed to a mellow luster by those sensitive hands. At times she felt the sexual tension radiating beneath that gentle fondling, but he'd kept it so damped down, she'd been aware of it only on a subliminal level. It was as if, since that first night in his suite, he'd been carefully preparing the ground, nurturing their relationship with humor and tenderness, sprinkling it with understanding, and protecting it from the brash intrusion of the weeds of dissension and uneasiness.

"I'm glad you don't wear a bra," he said, nuzzling her throat like an affectionate puppy. "Is it because I asked you not to?"

"I'd like to give your ego a lift and tell you it was," Billie said, her violet eyes twinkling. "But the truth is, I never wear one. I find them uncomfortable and I'm not big enough to really need one."

"And I thought it was because you liked my hands on you," David murmured, lifting and weighing her gently. He looked down at the mounds in his hands. "That you liked me to look at you." He chuckled mischievously as he saw the unmistakable tautening and swelling, and bent to kiss one breast tenderly before nestling his head against her contentedly. "You smell of lilacs too."

"I should; you put enough of it down there," she said, remembering with a sudden tingle of heat the way he'd stroked the crystal stopper of the vial of perfume teasingly over her bare breasts before bringing her close to rub against her with lazy sensuality.

"I like lilacs," he said logically, "and warm, sweet breasts, and soft, sensitive lips, and—"

"I think I get the message." She laughed.

"And I think you like me, too, don't you, windflower?"

How could she help it? she thought, with an odd tightening of her throat. He was so dear. Part mischievous little boy, part sage, and all golden, virile male. "You have your moments," she said huskily.

"And so do you," he said, his arms going around her and pulling her close. "And this is one of the special ones for both of us." He brushed his lips against her temple. "Let's just lie here and hold each other for a while. Doesn't this feel wonderful, Billie?"

"Wonderful," she agreed softly. The smell of lemon, musk, and spice; warm, strong arms; the crisp feel of the blue, oxford-cloth shirt beneath her cheek; the rich blur of Oriental rugs in the dim room . . . it was all so beautifully evocative, she could have stayed forever. "You're right. This is much better than the coppersmith's. Do you suppose we could stay here for an hour or so, or do you think Hassan would get suspicious?"

He didn't answer, his arms tightening about her with a possessiveness he'd never known. Always before when he'd cared for people, he'd been able to understand their need for personal freedom. He'd been able to let them go and let them flourish and develop and he'd known a joy just watching them grow and gain serenity and contentment. Bree, Alex, Karim, his parents—he'd never wanted to shackle them. Why, then, did he have to force himself to overcome an almost irresistible urge to possess and hold this woman in his arms, the one person who'd fight against that restraint more fiercely than anyone else?

Lying so docilely against him now, it seemed impossible to remember what a wary, independent, wild thing she really was. Yet even while she was here in his arms and he could feel the warm, loving tenderness of her reaching out to him, he knew she would panic and fly away if he didn't move with the greatest of care.

But he would move with care. He couldn't do anything else. Because he'd realized in that first moment what Billie was going to be to him. Recognized. Yes, that was the word. It was as if he'd known she was out there somewhere waiting for him, and when he'd finally caught sight of her on that hilltop, he'd felt a deep, serene sense of completion. It hadn't even surprised him. It was all a part of the beauty and rhythm of life. Part of the cycle that was as natural as growth and love itself. He'd just have to be patient and try to teach Billie the value of what they'd found together.

But he needed time, and he couldn't be sure when that wariness in her would trigger the restlessness that he knew was his worst enemy. At times he wondered if he should have taken her that first night and wrung at least a sexual commitment from her that might have bound her for a time. No, they both deserved more than that, and if he could channel desire and desperation into patience, they had a chance of getting it.

His clasp loosened reluctantly, and he pushed her away from him. "Much as I'd like to test old Hassan's patience to the limit, I'm afraid we're going to have to get back to the Casbah, sweetheart." He sat up and began deftly buttoning her shirt. "I'm expecting a package to be delivered by Karim's Marasef Express this afternoon and I'd like to make sure there's no slipup."

"Marasef Express?" Billie sat up and tucked her shirt firmly in her jeans and began to tidy her hair. "What on earth is that?"

"There's a helicopter landing pad on the grounds of the Casbah, and Karim has dispatches and deliveries arriving every few days from Alex and Bree"—his eyes twinkled—"as well as from sundry informants and corporate board members. So much for his so-called abdication."

"Clancy said he couldn't resist wheeling and dealing," Billie said. "I didn't know about the helicopter pad, though."

"How could you? You've been so busy running me ragged exploring Zalandan, you haven't had time to tour the Casbah and grounds."

"Tomorrow," she promised cheerfully as she took his hand and was pulled to her feet. "I gather you've had your fill of shopping for the time being?"

"Not necessarily. I think I'm developing a taste for it. Now which one of these rugs would you like?"

"I took the lilac perfume. I'm not about to accept a handwoven carpet," she said firmly.

"You wouldn't take the copper samovar either," he said sulkily. "I don't see why not. It couldn't have been all that valuable with that dent in it." He shrugged. "Oh, well, maybe I'll send it to Bree. She can always use an extra samovar."

"She can?" Billie asked skeptically. "Just what does one do with a samovar in this day and age?".

"Fill it with fruit? How do I know?" He made a face. "Bree will think of something." He was scanning the carpets hastily. "I think I'll take that ivory-and-slate Hariz. We've got to thank old Hassan some way for the use of his back room. I'll send it to my mother, in Texas. She likes that shade of blue."

"Your parents are still alive?" Billie asked, surprised. She couldn't remember his speaking of them at all the last three days. He'd been open and affectionate, sharing his memories and experiences with Alex, Bree, Karim, and the Rubinoffs as if he wanted her to know and love them as much as he did. But they were all experiences that were rooted in Sedikhan. It seemed he'd never lived any other life than the one he'd known here.

He nodded. "They still live on that ranch in the Rio Grande valley where I grew up." He took her elbow and was pushing her gently toward the paisley door hanging. For a moment there was a shadow on his face that could have been pain. "We don't get together much any more." Then the shadow was gone and he was grinning down at her. "You're sure you don't have a use for one slightly dented samovar? Where else could you get one with a personalized head print? I might even be persuaded to autograph it for you." His nonsense continued, and soon she was chuckling so hard, the memory of that fleeting pain on his face was lost in the sunlit spell he wove so well.

Yasmin was waiting in her suite when she arrived a little over an hour later; a worried frown on her usually serene brow signaled definite trouble. She was no sooner in the room than the housekeeper bustled forward, took her shoulder bag and packages, and gave her a nudge toward the bathroom.

"You must hurry," she said briskly. "I have laid out the dress you wore the first night you were here. You have only twenty minutes to bathe and change before he arrives."

"Before who arrives?" Billie asked blankly.

"Sheikh Karim," Yasmin answered, urging her through the door. "He sent word an hour ago that he wished to speak to you and would call on you in your apartment at six. He will be most displeased if he's kept waiting. It is not the custom, you understand."

"I can't see what the hurry is now," Billie said dryly as she unbuttoned her shirt and shrugged out of it. "The man's made no effort to see me in the three days I've been here. In fact, I've gotten the distinct impression he'd be delighted if I disappeared into the woodwork."

"That is not fair," Yasmin said, troubled. "The sheikh is a very conscientious host. If Lisan had not insisted on having you to himself and dining in his suite, I'm sure he would have done his duty."

"Duty," Billie repeated with a bittersweet smile. "Remind me to tell you how much that particular word turns me off. No one has to do their duty by me. Not any more." She was stripping quickly, Yasmin picking the clothes up as quickly as she discarded them. "And I'm not going to put on that dress again even to please your precious lord and master. The only reason I wore it was because I didn't have anything to wear. Now that I have my own clothes again, that's no longer necessary." She was carefully going down the three marble steps to the sunken tub. "If you want to help me dress, lay out something that belongs to me."

"There's nothing suitable." Yasmin sighed. "Sheikh Karim doesn't approve of women in trousers, and you have nothing else. I have never seen a woman without one dress in her wardrobe." She was almost wringing her hands. "It is most unseemly."

"I like jeans," Billie said with simple logic. "I'm comfortable in them, and I'm not the type of person who would tuck away a glamorous little black dress for that occasional night on the town. I don't even like dressing up and going out." Then, as Yasmin's despairing expression didn't change, she melted. She genuinely liked the dignified, if slightly autocratic, housekeeper, and she knew Yasmin would consider the blame hers if Billie wasn't presented in what she considered respectable attire. "Oh, all right," she said crossly. "I'll wear the blasted dress, but only until the sheikh leaves. Then off it comes. I'll dine with David in my jeans, as usual."

However, she'd only finished her bath and was slipping on a beige-and-black-striped jellaba she'd bought in the bazaar when Yasmin was back. "He's here," she hissed, hurriedly buttoning the loose robe herself as if Billie were a small child. "And very impatient." She smoothed Billie's tumbled curls frantically. "Hurry!" She gave Billie a push whose momentum sent her through the diaphanous curtains of the door.

"Charming." Karim Ben Raschid's voice was a silky purr as his eyes raked over her with the sharpness of a blade. He was standing by the filigreed doors that led to the little private balcony, and their fretted delicacy only accented the power and dominance of his robe-clad figure. "I'm sure you disapprove of compliments as much as you do hypocrisy, Miss Callahan, but I'm sure David has told you how much that jellaba suits you. It makes you look like one of the small children clamoring for coins in the bazaar."

Was there an insulting double-entendre in that? Probably, but she wasn't about to decipher it now. "I don't object to compliments," she said calmly as she came forward. "People like me need all they can get. I just insist they be founded on honesty." She gestured to the ivory-cushioned cane chair by the balcony door. "Why don't we sit down and get comfortable? I have an idea I may need all the support I can get."

He smiled, his strong white teeth a gleaming slash in his bearded face. "You may indeed, Miss Callahan," he said softly. "By all means make yourself comfortable. I believe I'll stand, however."

"As you like." Billie crossed to the bed, plopped down on the end, and crossed her legs tailor fashion. Her feet were still bare, she noticed wryly. No doubt that was an added touch of lese majesty. "I gather this is not a social call."

He shook his head. "We've already established that you dislike observing the amenities," he said. "I never repeat a mistake."

"Don't you?" Billie asked flippantly. "That must make you almost perfect by now. It must give you a great deal of satisfaction."

Karim's eyes narrowed. "Are you laughing at me, Miss Callahan?"

"Perhaps a little," she said, suddenly weary. "I have a tendency to laugh at what I'm afraid of. You're a very intimidating man, Sheikh Ben Raschid."

There was a flicker of surprise in his face. "You admit to weakness? That could be a very grave tactical error."

"Tactics are used in game plans," she answered, holding his gaze steadily. "I told you I don't play games." She tossed her head with barely restrained impatience. "Look, could we just get down to cases? I don't think you're here because you crave the pleasure of my company."

"I don't know why you should assume that." Karim lifted a mocking brow. "David seems to find your company pleasurable, even positively enthralling. Why should I not?"

"Oh, David." Her voice lowered to a guttural, tough-guy snarl. "But you know how it is, Pops. We hoods always have to set up our hits. We lull them into a false sense of security and then . . ." She pointed an index finger and pulled an imaginary trigger. "Gotcha."

"I don't regard that as amusing." The sheikh's tone was definitely chilly. "Not when it pertains to David."

"Neither do I," Billie said with a shiver she tried to hide with a careless shrug. "I told you I always laugh at things I'm afraid of. I'm sorry you didn't like my little charade."

"I'm sure you did it very well," Karim said coolly. "You appear to have a wide acquaintance with all strata of society, so I'm sure the vernacular came quite easily."

Billie stiffened warily. "Would you like to elaborate on that?"

"I'd be delighted." He moved a few feet to the cane chair and picked up an ivory folder that had blended in so well with the color of the cushion, she hadn't noticed it. "Shall we start with your appearance at the Simon Hardwicks Children's Home twenty-three years ago, or do you want me to zero in on your latest escapade at the location site at Marasef? It all makes very colorful reading."

"You've had me investigated." Billie's eyes widened. Why was she so surprised? It was a natural course of action for a man like Ben Raschid. Nevertheless it gave her a sense of being violated. "I'm glad my biography proved entertaining." She lifted her head proudly. "And I don't believe you've discovered anything particularly reprehensible. I'm not as dangerous as you supposed, am I?"

"Because you have no criminal record?" His

smile was enigmatic. "On the contrary, you could be even more dangerous than I thought." He opened the folder and glanced at it. "You're an extraordinary woman, Miss Callahan. My investigators are extremely competent men, and even they had a great deal of trouble filling in all the blanks. Your childhood was fairly easy. There were orphanage records substantiating the date you were turned over to them. You were a foundling, were you not?"

"Yes, I was," Billie answered steadily. "I'm not ashamed of my birth, Sheikh Ben Raschid. I believe it's what we make of ourselves that counts, not what we start out with as basic raw material."

"I meant no insult." The sheikh shrugged. "I have similar beliefs, Miss Callahan. It's what you've made of yourself that holds my entire interest."

He scanned the page before him idly. "You were in several foster homes over the years. You ran away from two and were returned to the orphanage once for rebellious and uncooperative behavior. You ran away from the orphanage itself when you were fifteen. After that the trail becomes considerably more muddied."

"Sorry about that," Billie said ironically.

"Practically all the people you worked for, individuals whom you befriended, clammed up on my investigators," Ben Raschid said thoughtfully. "You seem to have the ability to attract enormous affection and loyalty in an amazingly short space of time." His eyes narrowed. "Because you've never stayed anywhere for more than a few months, have you, Miss Callahan? You've been a gas-station attendant, a file clerk, a cook in a lumber camp, you've picked apples in Oregon, worked on an

Indian reservation in Washington. The list appears to go on forever. You even went to college for a semester in California. You scored very high on the entrance exams, and your professors describe you as hard-working and exceptionally bright."

"The key phrase is hard-working," Billie said. "I may be a gypsy, but I've never been out for a free ride, and there's nothing in that report I'm ashamed to admit to."

"It was a surprisingly innocuous report for such a busy young lady," he said calmly. "No sexual liaisons, a few mischievous pranks, but nothing malicious. Nothing in the least suspicious until you arrived at the movie set in Marasef."

She straightened. "*Desert Venture*?" She shook her head. "You've been had, Sheikh Ben Raschid. Your boys must have decided to do a little fabricating to earn their fee. The only thing criminal about my work on that movie was the money I stole for my terrible performance."

"Not criminal, just suspicious," he said, closing the folder. "It seems you're a very brave lady, Miss Callahan. At some risk to yourself, you rescued a certain bordello bouncer by the name of Yusef Ibraheim from three toughs who were allegedly trying to slit his throat. You then set up a *ménage à trois* with this Yusef and a stunt woman, Kendra Michaels, in a two-room cottage and maintained the relationship for a number of weeks."

"*Ménage à trois!*" Billie exclaimed. "It was no such thing. We were friends, damn it. Your investigators have very dirty minds, Sheikh Ben Raschid."

"Perhaps. But you can't deny you've been living with this Yusef at his home in a village near Zalandan for some time."

"With Yusef, his parents, and sundry brothers and sisters," Billie said indignantly. "It was hardly the cozy little love nest you're implying. What difference does it make, anyway? My morals are my own business. I haven't been cross-examining you about your sex life."

For a minute there was a glint of amusement in Ben Raschid's eyes. "I haven't the slightest doubt you would do so if it suited your fancy." His face darkened in a frown. "Your morals are no concern of mine. There are ways of insuring fidelity if you became important to David. You can be sure there would be no more affairs once he decided he wanted you."

"Chastity belts, seraglios, eunuch guards with curved scimitars?" Billie scoffed. "This is the twentieth century, haven't you heard? Lord, I can't believe any of this."

"Nothing so primitive and uncivilized," Ben Raschid said with a tigerish smile. "I'm a very civilized man, Miss Callahan."

"You and Attila the Hun." Billie snorted.

"I've been called a barbarian to my face before," the sheikh said with soft menace, "but not by anyone who is still around." He tossed the folder on the chair. "All this is beside the point. I told you your personal affair with Ibraheim was not important—it's your business relationship that concerns me."

"Business relationship?" Billie asked blankly.

"I find it an odd coincidence that you should make the acquaintance of an employee of a bordello," Ben Raschid said slowly. "It makes me wonder what other contacts you have in that area. I believe you've been told Ladram's crime ring was into vice as well."

"Oh, no." Billie groaned. "Now I'm a candidate for the position of madam of a bordello. What will you think of next?"

"I didn't say that, I just said it was a curious coincidence."

"And you and Clancy and all your errand boys don't like coincidences," she said gloomily. "I've heard that line before. Just what *is* the purpose of this little visit, Sheikh Ben Raschid? Are you trying to intimidate me into going away and leaving David alone? I don't like scare tactics. I'll leave when I'm ready, not before."

Ben Raschid shrugged. "I don't know quite why I came here today. Perhaps to gauge your reaction to the report. Perhaps I just wanted to study you and see what David sees in you that appeals to him." His face was suddenly weary. "Whether you go or stay is David's decision after he reads the copy of the report I sent him."

Billie froze. "You sent a copy to David?"

"Of course. As soon as it arrived by helicopter this afternoon, I had a copy made and sent to his apartment." His narrowed eyes were studying her face. "He's probably read it by now. Does that upset you?"

It did upset her. It angered her far more than the thought of Ben Raschid or Clancy prying into the details of her private life, which was totally irrational. But then, why did she have to be rational or logical? That was for the Karims and Clancys of this world. She'd be as emotional and irrational as she damn well wanted to be!

"Yes, it upsets me," she said between her teeth. "I'm sick and tired of being treated like some kind of criminal." She uncrossed her legs, jumped off the bed, and strode to the rosewood bureau across the room. "I didn't ask to be dropped into the middle of your problems, and I'll be damned if I'll have my life stripped bare to interest your precious Lisan." She was pulling jeans, a tunic top, and underthings haphazardly out of the drawers. "And I'm about to tell him so." She marched toward the bath/dressing-room area. "Good day, Sheikh Ben Raschid. This audience is officially at an end. Please close the door on your way out."

The folder was lying open on the rosewood desk, and David looked up, unsurprised, as she stormed into the room without knocking. "Hello, windflower. I've been expecting you." He glanced down at the paper before him. "Did you really apprentice as a clown in a circus? You must have enjoyed that."

"Yes, I really did that," she mimicked as she strode over to the desk and picked up the folder. "And I really did all the rest of it too. You'll be happy to know your investigators are very thorough." Her violet eyes were blazing. "Of course, they have the minds of sewer rats, but that's incidental, isn't it? It must have provided you with some titillating predinner reading." She drew a deep breath. "Well, I think it's absolutely disgusting. This is my life you're scanning so casually. How would you like it if I nosed around in your past, interrogating your friends and digging into records about a kid who doesn't even exist any more?"

"But I believe she does exist," David said quietly, a flicker of sadness in his eyes. "I think that little girl is very much alive. And I think you know the investigation wasn't my idea. I hope I would have found out all this myself in time."

"Yet you didn't hesitate to read the report."

"Yes, I read it." He leaned back in the chair and regarded her steadily. "I would have had to be a saint to resist the temptation to find out everything I could about you when it was right at my fingertips. I won't even try to lie and tell you I thought you wouldn't mind. I knew you'd be mad as hell at me for reading it."

"You're damn right I am."

"You have the right to be indignant, of course. An invasion of privacy is a serious breach of friendship." He took the file from her clenched hand and dropped it into the rattan wastebasket by the desk. "However, you're more than indignant, you're furious. Perhaps even out of proportion to the crime itself. Have you asked yourself why you're reacting so violently? You're a gypsy who skims the surface of life. Why should the fact that I know about that scared little girl matter so much?"

"I wasn't scared," she said quickly. "I was never frightened. I was too tough for that. Orphanage brats have to be. You read the report. Rebellious and uncooperative. Does that sound like a pathetic Orphan Annie?"

"No, it sounds like my strong, loving Billie striking out at something she doesn't understand. It sounds like loneliness and despair and hurt." His eyes were strangely bright. "God, I wish I'd been there to hold you and help you through it."

"I didn't need any help," she said defiantly. "Not after I understood the system. I learned very quickly how the world worked." She shrugged. "Those people who fostered me couldn't help it because they couldn't love me. They had families of their own, and I wasn't exactly Shirley Temple. I was scrawny, with fiery orange braids, and so shy I was afraid to say boo. They only did it for the welfare money and they *did* do their duty." Her lips twisted. "I remember Mrs. Anders saying that when she took me back to the orphanage that last time. She told the matron they'd done their duty, but Billie was just too difficult to handle. Next time they wanted a more docile child." She lifted her chin. "They stopped trying to place me after that."

As he thought of that vulnerable, proud, lonely Billie with a spirit so full of love and no one to give it to, he felt an aching protectiveness so intense, it was an actual physical pain. He wanted to reach out and touch, to cradle and soothe away the pain he could feel beneath that brash defensiveness. His hands clenched unconsciously to keep himself from doing just that. Not yet. He could see how finely balanced on the edge of uncertainty and fear she was. Afraid to trust, afraid to love, afraid to give herself for more than a moment. A loving nature so strong it had to give, but so afraid that love wouldn't be returned that she refused to linger and chance rejection. *Stay, windflower. Put down roots and let me show you that love doesn't always go away.* He slowly unclenched his fists and drew a deep breath. Not yet.

"It would probably have been like trying to place a tiger cub with a household of tabbies," he said lightly. "Who could blame them for wanting to keep a fierce little gypsy like you under lock and key?" He could see the tension ease out of her.

"I wasn't all that bad," she said with a reluctant smile. "I just hated the idea of being a charity child. If they left me alone, I was even fairly civilized." Then the smile faded from her face and she scowled. "All of that's not really important. What's relevant here is that blasted dossier."

"That 'blasted' dossier has gone into the wastebasket, and that's where it will stay," he said quietly. "Anything else will come only from you. You have my promise." He smiled coaxingly, and she could feel the warmth begin to tingle through her. "Are you going to forgive me, Billie?"

There was no question of that, she thought helplessly. He was so disarming, she could feel the anger vanish as if it had never been. "I suppose so," she said grudgingly. "But that doesn't go for those protective lions you have prowling around you. They can just keep their noses out of my affairs. I've had it with being a suspect for everything from murder to vice queen of Marasef."

He gave a whoop of laughter. "Poor baby, did he accuse you of that too?"

"Well, almost," she said, her lips quirking. "I'm not sure if even he could find me plausible in that role. I think he was just a little upset that I'd called him a barbarian."

"Karim would definitely take umbrage at that." David's eyes were dancing. "He's been trying to civilize that strain of barbarism out of his character since he was a kid. It's not exactly safe to hint that he's not been very successful."

"I gathered that." She shrugged. "Oh, well, he won't have to put up with me for very long. You did say the mechanic had almost finished repairing my Jeep."

"Almost." David's smile vanished. "This afternoon the helicopter should have brought the part he needed to fix it."

The sudden jab of pain she felt made no sense at all. "Then I'll probably be on my way in a day or so," she said lightly. "And Karim and Clancy can breathe a joint sigh of relief."

There was a flicker of some unidentifiable emotion on his face before it was masked. "Something else arrived on the helicopter besides the replacement part," he said as he pushed back his chair and stood up.

"That package you were expecting?"

He nodded. "It's something in the nature of a replacement too." He was crossing to the carved teak armoire, and glanced over his shoulder as he opened the door and reached inside. "It's a present, and I'm not taking no for an answer this time. I don't have anyone else I can give it to."

"I told you I wasn't accepting any—" She broke off as she saw what he had in his hands. A Spanish guitar, so exquisite that it was a true work of art, the mellow golden wood silkened to a warm, glowing patina.

But no more glowing than David's eyes as he carried it across the room and halted before her. He held the lovely thing out to her with a gentle smile. "It's a very good guitar. I know it's not your old friend, but, given time, perhaps it can be a new one." He frowned uncertainly as he saw the look of shock on her face as she stared at the guitar as if she couldn't tear her gaze away. "It's not really a replacement, Billie. I've sent the old one to Madrid to have the major surface damage repaired. There's no way the sound would ever be the same without practically rebuilding it, and I didn't think you'd want that. I thought you'd rather set it somewhere in a place of honor, with all its honorable patches intact." When she still didn't speak, his frown deepened. "Billie?"

She reached out slowly and touched the guitar with a hesitant finger. "It's beautiful," she said huskily, "so beautiful." And she wasn't speaking only of the guitar. She felt as if she were breaking apart inside. Such a wonderful, caring thing to do. "I love it." She drew a deep, shaky breath, and the eyes she lifted to his were starry with tears. "And you're right, I want to keep my honorable patches."

The worried frown disappeared. "That's all right, then," he said with a relieved sigh. "I was afraid I'd blown it."

"No." The word was a broken little murmur as she suddenly pushed the guitar aside and came into his arms like a little girl searching for home. "Oh, no." The word held an element of desperation as her arms slid around him and her head nestled against his shoulder. The tears she could no longer hold back were dampening the crispness of his blue oxford shirt. "No one's ever done anything so beautiful for me before. Please, I want to give you something. Let me give you something too. What do you want?"

She heard his chuckle reverberate beneath her ear as his free arm slid around her. "That's a hell of a question to ask a man who's verging on sexual starvation. I'm tempted to give you the age-old answer, but I detest clichés."

She could feel the color rise in her cheeks, and that only bewildered her more. She had never been this unsure before, and with David it was even more perplexing. She'd always felt so natural and at ease with him. "Don't joke. I mean it."

His hand reached up to stroke the tumbled curls at the nape of her neck. "I know you do," he said softly. "You can't bear to take and not give back, can you, Billie?" His fingers were beneath her hair now and massaging the neck muscles. "Don't worry, I'm going to let you give me a present. Something I want very much."

"What is it?"

"Stay with me for a little longer, windflower. That's what you can give me." His voice was a velvet croon in her ear. She felt the light touch of his lips on her ear, and his warm breath was like a caress in itself. "There are so many things we haven't been able to do together yet."

"You mean . . ."

He laughed softly. "The blossoming? Oh, yes, I meant that too. But I meant other things as well. We've never worked side by side. I've never shown you my garden. We've never ridden in the desert at dawn." He pushed her away to gaze down at her with a tender little smile. "And I've never heard you play a guitar or sing one of those songs you told me you make up. I want all those things very much. Will you give them to me?"

She nodded, blinking furiously to stop those idiotic tears from falling. "I'll stay for a while." She laughed shakily. "Though you may be getting more than you've bargained for. You've never heard me sing. Olivia Newton-John I'm not."

He carefully kept the relief from his face. Another reprieve. Another step closer. "I won't mind," he said with an easy grin. "I've been accused of being tone-deaf anyway." He stepped back and handed her the guitar with a mocking little bow. "Just make noise and I'll be happy."

"Noise," she said indignantly. "I'm not that terrible either." She ran her fingers over the strings in a loving caress. "It's so lovely."

"Why don't you sit down and get acquainted with your new friend?" he suggested. "I have some revisions I want to do on the new book. We'll send for dinner later."

"I'd like that," she said absently, kicking off her shoes on the way to the wide bed across the room.

She settled cross-legged on the end, frowning in concentration as she began to tune the guitar.

David shook his head in rueful amusement. He was already forgotten, and it seemed likely that condition would last for some time. He dropped down in the desk chair and cast one more glance at the shining copper head bent so eagerly over the graceful instrument. Then he clicked on the type-writer and his eyes narrowed in concentration as he, too, became lost in the rich garden of words and characters that was as absorbing for him as Billie's new friend was for her.

Five

Billie was humming softly as she opened the door to her suite carrying her guitar with the care her treasure deserved. It had been a lovely evening, she thought dreamily, and as unusual as the other moments spent with David Bradford. Unusual? There had been nothing really extraordinary about those hours in David's suite. She'd spent the time playing her guitar and composing snatches of songs for her own amusement while David worked on his book. He'd only thrown her an absent-minded word or smile a few times during the hours she was there, and they'd never gotten around to eating dinner. It was the warm, silent intimacy that had made those hours so precious. She'd paused a few times just to gaze at his intent face bent over the typewriter, lingering on the leashed tension pulling the blue shirt taut over his broad shoulders. There was an undercurrent of restrained excitement about him as he was caught up in his story that caused a surge of maternal tenderness to flow through her.

"I have been waiting for you. There is something you should know." Yasmin rose gracefully from the cane chair, a worried frown creasing her forehead.

Billie's eyes widened in surprise. "Don't tell me the sheikh wants to see me again," she said with an impish grin. "I didn't think he'd be able to put up with me twice in one day." She tilted her nose in mock hauteur. "You'll have to tell his royal arrogance that I'm no longer receiving tonight."

"No, it's not the sheikh," Yasmin said, biting her lower lip worriedly. "It is something that I heard from one of the guards. There is much gossip in the Casbah, but I think this is probably true." She ran her hand distractedly through her smoothly coiffed hair. "I did not know what to do."

Billie's smiled faded as she slowly crossed the room to lean her guitar in the corner closest to the bed. "Then, why don't you tell me what you've heard and we'll try to decide together?"

"Sheikh Karim is holding your friend prisoner," Yasmin blurted out in a hurried rush.

"What friend?" Billie asked bewilderedly as she dropped down on the bed. "What are you talking about?"

"An enormous giant of a man," Yasmin said quietly. "With long, wild hair and the strength of ten."

"Yusef," Billie identified him gloomily. "Oh, Lord, I might have known he'd follow me."

"Yes, that is his name. Yusef Ibraheim," Yasmin said. "He appeared at the Casbah this evening and demanded to see you. The guard said he was most belligerent."

"He would be." Billie sighed. "He seems to think I can't function without him to take care of me." She stiffened as Yasmin's other statement sank in. "They're holding him prisoner?"

Yasmin nodded unhappily. "He was in the library a long time with Sheikh Karim and Mr. Donahue, and then the guards were given orders to take him to the Silver Crescent and keep him prisoner until Sheikh Karim gives the word that he be released."

"Silver Crescent? What is that?"

"It's a place for evening entertainment, a café. You would call it a nightclub. It's about five minutes' journey from here. Sheikh Karim owns it, as he does most of Zalandan. He uses the back rooms for meetings and other activities when he requires more secrecy than the Casbah affords."

"Or when he decides to imprison an innocent man on a whim," Billie added grimly. "I can't believe it. Who does he think he is?"

"I'm sure the sheikh had good reason for doing what he did," Yasmin said cautiously. "Your friend will come to no harm if he's free from guilt."

"And who's to decide that?" Billie asked caustically. "Karim is evidently judge, jury, and executioner in Zalandan." She shivered suddenly. They wouldn't really hurt Yusef, would they? But Karim was something of a barbarian, and he was an absolute fanatic about David's safety. Yusef's employment in that bordello was a possible link with Ladram that might incriminate him in Karim's eyes. "I've got to get him out of there."

"No!" Yasmin shook her head adamantly. "That would be very dangerous. Perhaps if you went to the sheikh and pleaded for—"

"Pleaded," Billie echoed indignantly. "The man's a dictator. Do you think I'm going begging on my knees for him to release a man who shouldn't have been imprisoned in the first place? No, I'll get him out on my own."

"Then go to Lisan. He will use his influence with the sheikh."

"I'm not involving David," Billie said, jumping to her feet. "Yusef is my responsibility, and I'll take care of this myself. Tonight."

"Why not wait until tomorrow?" Yasmin said coaxingly. "One night can't hurt, and you may change your mind and decide to go to the sheikh after all."

"Tonight." Billie was at the bureau drawers, rummaging rapidly through them. "Yusef won't sit tamely by to be held prisoner, and he's so ferocious-looking, his guards are bound to be afraid of him. Fear breeds violence. I have to get him out tonight." She glanced up. "Where's the jellaba I was wearing earlier? It has a hood that may shadow my face." She pulled out a pair of khaki slacks. "These will probably do if that café is dim enough. It will be better if I can pass as a man. From what I've seen in the streets in the last few days, a woman alone would be too suspicious."

"The jellaba is in the dressing room," Yasmin answered absently. "You're going to free your friend by force?"

"If I don't find any other way. I'll play it by ear once I've reached the Silver Crescent."

Yasmin shook her head incredulously. "I would never have told you if I'd known you would do something so foolish. I thought you would go directly to Lisan and let him solve your problem."

"I solve my own problems," Billie said briskly. The black tunic shirt was large enough to disguise her small breasts, she decided, and her short suede boots would be masculine enough. "We do things differently where I come from." Suddenly she turned, and her eyes narrowed with curiosity. "Why did you run the risk of telling me about Yusef, Yasmin? You know the sheikh will be furious if he finds out you've warned me. I know how much your position in this household means to you."

"It is my life." Yasmin's gaze was steady. "Being in charge of the sheikh's residences is considered a great honor in Sedikhan. I've worked to reach that goal ever since I was a child."

"Then why?"

"Lisan," Yasmin said simply. "You have value in his eyes, and it would make him unhappy to see you sad or worried."

"And that means more to you than your position or your loyalty to Sheikh Karim?"

"It means everything." Yasmin's eyes were oddly bright. "Whatever happens, Lisan must not be made sad. I cared too much for my position once before and almost lost my Zilah. Lisan saved her. I will not hold it so dear again."

"Zilah?" Billie asked gently.

Yasmin's serene features were suddenly strained and white with pain, her lips tight to control their trembling. "My daughter, Zilah," she said. "Lisan did not tell you of Zilah?"

Billie shook her head. "I didn't know you had any children."

"There is only Zilah." Yasmin drew a shaky breath. "I'm not married, you see. Zilah is illegitimate. I understand that this is not such a shameful thing in your country now, but in Sedikhan it's a very serious transgression. She was born when I was thirty and had given up hope of finding love." She smiled sadly. "I found it, but the man was a foreigner, and married as well. I had to find a way of both supporting my Zilah and keeping my position with the sheikh."

"Wouldn't the sheikh have helped you?" Billie asked.

"I couldn't risk it. My shame was great in the eyes of my people. I kept Zilah's birth a secret and sent her to my mother in Marasef to be raised. I visited her whenever possible and sent her as much money as I could, to make sure that Zilah had a happy life." She shook her head. "I should have been there to protect her. I should have kept her with me."

"You did what you could," Billie said, her eyes warm with sympathy. "That's all any of us can do, Yasmin."

"It was not enough. My mother was old and did not keep close enough guard on her. Marasef can be a very wicked city for those who aren't protected." Yasmin closed her eyes, and her voice was a broken murmur. "Zilah disappeared one day. She was such a pretty little girl, so bright and shining. We knew what had happened to her." Yasmin's lids flicked open, and her eyes were dark with agony. "I was frantic. I did everything I could think of. The police. Searching the streets myself. Everything. Six months had passed and there was no sign of her. And then I told Lisan." She smiled sadly. "I did not mean to, but he could see I was worried, and it all came tumbling out. Thank Allah I told Lisan."

"What did he do?" Billie asked, almost unbearably moved by the pain on Yasmin's face.

"He found her and brought her to me," she said simply. "He went to Marasef and searched until he found her. She was in a house of shame, as we had thought. They had drugged her with heroin and kept her addicted so that she would be docile and comply with the way they were using her." Her voice was vibrant with agony. "My Zilah was only thirteen years old!"

"Oh, my God." Billie could feel her own throat tighten with tears. "My God."

"Have you ever seen anyone suffer from heroin addiction? It is a terrible thing. Not only for the addict, but for the people who are trying to help. I wasn't strong enough to help her, but Lisan was. Lisan stayed with her while she suffered withdrawal symptoms that tore her apart. We gave her methadone, but the suffering was still a horror to watch." Her face was a frozen mask of pain. "And when she was better, it was even worse, because she began to remember what had happened in that house. She felt ugly and used, and the nightmares were terrible. Lisan stayed with her then too. He filled her room with plants and flowers; he brought her huge bouquets of balloons. He surrounded her with color and caring and he held her hand and listened." The tears were running down her cheeks in a slow trickle. "I could not listen. I tried, but I couldn't do it. But Lisan listened, and gradually the pain poured into him and the ugliness vanished as if it had never been. Because in Lisan's eyes she could see that she was still the beautiful child she had always been." There was a moment of silence in the room more poignant than the words that had gone before. Then Yasmin shook her head as if to clear it of the painful memories and tried to smile. "Yes, Lisan's happiness means much to me. There is very little I wouldn't do to insure it."

"I can see that," Billie said huskily, blinking rapidly to keep back the tears. "Where is Zilah now?"

"The doctor said it would be better to send Zilah far away from the site of her memories. Lisan sent her to America to people who will love and care for her." She smiled sadly. "I miss her very much but it is best. She writes me, and her letters are content—and even happy sometimes."

"I'm glad," Billie said softly. "I'm so glad, Yasmin."

"So am I," Yasmin said simply, her dark eyes serene now. "And if helping you will make Lisan happy, then I must do it. It is because of my Zilah that he is in danger now. When Zilah left for America, he went back to Marasef. I had never seen Lisan angry before, but he was angry then." She shivered. "It was a terrible, burning anger. He went to Alex Ben Raschid and together they destroyed the network that had preyed upon children like my Zilah."

"No," Billie said decidedly. "I can't let you involve yourself more than you have already. You can help me dress and take me to this Silver Crescent if you like, but after that I'm on my own. You come directly back to the Casbah and wait until I get back."

"But I wish—"

"No," Billie repeated gently but firmly as she carried her armload of clothes toward the dressing room. "Yusef is my responsibility, and I'll take care of this on my own."

"The guard says they will probably keep your friend in the office in the back," Yasmin said as she drew deeper into the shadowy doorway of the tiny shop across the street from the Silver Crescent. "The second green door."

"Right." Billie checked the pins in her hair to be

sure they were secure and drew the hood over her head so that it shadowed her face. "I'll be fine now. You go on back to the Casbah."

"I don't know," Yasmin said hesitantly. "Perhaps . . ."

"Go," Billie said firmly. She bent forward to brush the other woman's cheek in an affectionate kiss. "Thank you." Then she was striding across the cobbled street with what she hoped was a mannish gait and opening the door of the café.

She was immediately met with a blast of smoke and the music of zilaks and cymbals in a throbbing Eastern rhythm. It was so dark she could barely make out the outline of the tables and the shapes of the robed figures that were seated at them. The only light was focused on the voluptuous figure of the belly dancer gyrating in the center of the dance floor, and the attention of everyone in the room appeared to be riveted on her shaking hips. It was no wonder, Billie thought wryly. How on earth did she keep that little bit of material from vibrating off? It had to be glued on. Well, the darkness and the floor show were definitely to her advantage, and she'd better use that distraction to get to the back office. Now, where the devil was it?

Ah, an arched doorway with its curtain of beads was barely visible a short distance from the dance floor. She made her way carefully among the close-packed tables. As she passed a vacant one she absently spotted an empty tray and a large white towel carelessly left by one of the waiters. What could be more natural in a café than a waiter? And what could be more inviting to two guards than a bottle of wine? She snatched up the tray and draped the white towel over her left arm. That made a nice, authentic touch. Now for the wine.

She stopped at a table occupied by two bearded men who seemed particularly entranced by the belly dancer's navel and matter-of-factly picked up their half-empty glasses and put them on the tray. Then she reached for the bottle of wine in the center of the table.

Her hand was immediately gripped protestingly. Evidently the threat of the absence of liquid beverage was more important than the belly dancer's charms. Her hand tightened on the neck of the bottle.

"Bad," she croaked hoarsely in Arabic. She grabbed her throat and stuck her tongue out like someone in the last extremities of poisoning. "Botulism." Was that the same medical word in Sedikhan? Evidently it was, because the man snatched his hand away from the bottle as if he'd been burned and clutched fearfully at his own throat. She set the bottle on the tray. Poor man. As she picked up the tray and turned toward the beaded curtain, she added tersely in Arabic, "Maybe." At least he had hope now.

The second green door. She paused before it and drew a deep, steadying breath. She adjusted the hood again and licked her lips nervously. It was dim here in the hall, but there was a light beneath the door that indicated she would have no such luck once she was in the room. She'd just have to keep her head down and pretend to be a very servile waiter. She balanced the tray on her hip as she spilled the remaining wine in the glasses on the floor and wiped them with her towel. Draping the towel back over her arm and not letting herself think, she knocked peremptorily on the door.

There was a murmur of voices, followed by the sound of chairs being pushed back. Then the door was flung open and she was facing a young soldier in the now-familiar olive-green uniform. No guns, she noticed with relief.

"Wine," she croaked in Arabic. "From Sheikh Karim Ben Raschid."

Oh, Lord, there was a look of surprise on the young soldier's face. Evidently the sheikh didn't approve of his men drinking on the job. "One glass," she growled sternly. The surprise faded and the soldier stepped back, glancing back to call something over his shoulder to his cohort at the table across the room. She gathered it was less than complimentary to the sheikh and a trifle ungrateful.

She glided forward, her head bent, darting glances around the room from beneath her lashes. Yusef was there, she noted with relief. He was sitting in the executive chair behind the desk, bound efficiently with strong ropes. The two guards had evidently been playing cards at the table across the room, for there was an ashtray overflowing with cigarette butts and a pile of chips in the center of the table. The other guard at the table had no handgun either, and her swift gaze spotted two rifles propped against the wall by the desk. Thank heavens luck was on the side of the righteous tonight.

She heard the door close behind her as she headed briskly for the desk. She put the tray down and fussed with the glasses a moment, peering beneath her lashes at Yusef. He didn't seem hurt or abused in any way, but as he glared at the men across the room, there was a fierce scowl on his roughhewn face that was so intimidating, she couldn't really blame the guards for binding those Samson-like shoulders so heavily. Dressed in voluminous dark trousers shoved into suede boots and a white, long-sleeved shirt stretched across the mighty biceps of his chest, he resembled an Arabian Nights genie captured in a sorcerer's enchanted bonds. The guard who'd opened the door was now dropping back into his chair and picking up his cards. She drew a deep breath and could feel her heart start to pound. It was now or never.

She whirled and dashed for the rifles against the wall. She'd snatched up one when she heard a shout from the table behind her and the screech of chairs shoved hurriedly back. Then she was turning and pointing the rifle at the guards with what she hoped appeared to be lethal competence. "Stop," she shouted, her finger on the trigger. "Stay." Oh, damn, that sounded like a canine command. How could you sound dangerous when you only knew a little Arabic?

Evidently they were too stunned to take offense at the command and too wary of the barrel of the rifle pointed at them to disobey her. So far, so good. "I'll have you untied in a minute, Yusef," she called, shaking her head so the hood fell to her shoulders.

"You shouldn't be here," Yusef said sternly. "There is danger. Go away and I will crush these vermin on my own."

"That's very ungrateful, Yusef," she said indignantly, her eyes glued warily on the two guards. "Would Luke Skywalker say a thing like that if Princess Leia came to his rescue?"

"Luke Skywalker?"

"Never mind." She sighed. "I guess the *Star Wars* saga hasn't reached Sedikhan yet."

"You shouldn't have come here," Yusef growled. "Go away before you are hurt."

"Oh, be quiet, Yusef," she said with exasperation. "Don't I have enough to worry about without your nagging me? Can't you be rescued with good grace, for heaven's sake?" The boyish-faced guard took a sudden step forward, and she hurriedly lifted the drooping rifle. "Stay!"

He stayed. Maybe she was more dangerous-looking than she thought. Now to get those ropes off Yusef. Why hadn't she thought to bring a knife? She searched for something to use as a substitute and noticed the wine bottle. Jagged glass.

She grabbed the neck of the bottle and, keeping an eagle eye on the two guards, backed around the desk until she was standing beside Yusef's chair. Cradling the rifle in her arm she brought the bottle down on the edge of the desk with a crash. It didn't break.

"They always break," she muttered incredulously. "I've never seen a movie where the bottle didn't break." She crashed the bottle down again. A long crack appeared, but it still didn't shatter. "What the hell is it made of?"

"Wouldn't it be easier to try to find a letter-opener in the desk?" David asked from the doorway. "I'm sure it would be much less messy, windflower."

"What are you doing here?" she asked, startled. Then she answered her own question. "Yasmin."

He nodded as he strolled into the room. "She couldn't take the chance you might be hurt, so she came running to me for help." He grinned as he took in the slight figure with the rifle cradled in her arm. "I don't think she would be quite so concerned if she could see you now."

"I don't need any help." She was opening the desk drawers frantically and finally found the letter-opener. It appeared to have a fairly sharp blade, she noticed with satisfaction, and proceeded to saw through the thick rope.

The young guard suddenly took a step toward David. "Lisan, we have orders to keep this man under guard. You must stop her."

"She appears very determined, Abdul," David drawled, his eyes dancing. "I think we'd better let her have her way."

"*Let* me." She snorted. Suddenly the rope was cut through and Yusef was tearing the coils from around himself. "I don't see that there's a choice. Come on, Yusef. You go ahead. I'll cover them."

Muttering something beneath his breath, he strode quickly across the room. She followed closely, her gaze on the younger guard, who seemed to be gathering himself to spring.

However, it wasn't Abdul, but the older guard, who took advantage of her distractedness to leap toward her with all the lethal menace of a Green Beret and knock the rifle from her hand.

"No!"

She heard David's sharp cry but didn't see the blur of movement as he crossed the room. Abdul had also sprung toward her now, and she felt a thrill of fear as she saw his grimly determined face. Suddenly David was there, a swift karate chop on the neck making Abdul drop like a stone, and a well-placed kick in the loins causing the other guard to double over with a bellow of pain.

"Come on," he said grimly, turning and grabbing her by the elbow. "We'd better get out of here. I don't think when they recover they're going to be too pleased with us."

Then the three of them were running down the hall, through the smoke-hazed café, toward the front entrance. She was vaguely conscious of the shouts of the patrons at the tables and the outraged squeal of the belly dancer as they ran across the dance floor in front of her.

The cool night air hit them as they tore out the door, and then they were dashing down the narrow, winding street, their footsteps loud on the cobblestones. They were almost three blocks away from the Silver Crescent when David called a halt and pulled them both into the dimly lit vestibule of an apothecary shop.

They were all breathing in harsh gasps and Billie leaned against the rough concrete wall with a sigh of relief. "Do you think we're safe?"

"Well, I haven't heard any sounds of pursuit," David answered. "I think we would on these cobblestones." He glanced at the other man. "I don't believe we've been introduced," he said politely, his lips twitching. "My name is David Bradford and I believe you must be Yusef Ibraheim."

Yusef nodded. "Lisan," he said quietly. "I've heard of you in the bazaars. It took me a day of questioning to find out where Billie had been taken."

"I wasn't taken anywhere," Billie said. "I went to the Casbah voluntarily, and I'm quite safe there." She scowled. "I think."

"You are," David said, brushing a lock of hair from her forehead. "You'll always be safe anywhere that I am, Billie."

"Very nice to hear." She made a face. "You might tell that to Karim. He doesn't make me feel any too secure."

"I will," he said, his face grave. "I'm sorry this

happened, Billie. I promise nothing like it will happen again."

"You're damn right it won't," she said crossly. "Because Yusef is leaving Zalandan tonight, and as soon as my Jeep is repaired, I'll be on my way too."

"No," Yusef said stubbornly. "I will not leave you alone in that place. You will come with me tonight."

"I can't leave the Jeep," she said impatiently. "It doesn't belong to me. I only borrowed it from the production company of *Desert Venture.* I'll be perfectly all right, Yusef. Karim is only worried about David's safety. If he doesn't think I'm on the verge of murdering him, he won't make any moves against me."

"I will not go away," Yusef growled.

"Neither one of you is going anywhere," David said with quiet certainty. "You're both coming back to the Casbah with me. There's no need for either one of you to run away. I told you that. I can handle Karim."

"After tonight?" she asked, raising a skeptical eyebrow. "Even if I wanted to jeopardize Yusef's freedom, it would be too big a risk after what happened at the Silver Crescent. I don't believe Karim's a man who likes to have his arrangements upset."

"There's no risk." David's face was stern and set in the dim light. "I'll keep you both safe. Trust me, Billie. Tonight you promised you'd give me time, that you'd stay with me for a little while." He reached out to stroke the curve of her cheek with a tenderness so exquisite it started an ache of response deep within her. "Are you going to break your word?"

"But Yusef—"

"Will be safe *and* free," David interrupted, his eyes holding hers. "Won't you trust me?"

A gentle finger stroking a scarred guitar, a room full of flowers and gay balloons, a strong man holding the hand of a child in pain and taking on that pain himself. The memories rushed over her in an overwhelming golden tide. She felt her throat tighten and the tears brim helplessly in her eyes. How could she help but give her trust to a man like that?

"Yes, I trust you," she said huskily. She turned to Yusef. "We're going back to the Casbah with David."

Six

They had scarcely entered the foyer of the Casbah when they were met by a fiercely frowning Clancy Donahue. "Well, Billie. You certainly played hell this evening." His gaze raked over Yusef with a flicker of surprise. "You really did break him out. When Abdul called from the café, he was practically incoherent, mumbling something about wine and a spitfire of a *lallah* who held them at gunpoint." His lips tightened grimly as he glanced at David. "You appeared rather prominently in his report too. I didn't teach you karate so you could use it against our own men, David."

"It was necessary," David said simply. "They tried to attack Billie."

"From what I heard, she was the one doing the attacking," Clancy said dryly. "But at least you had the sense to bring them back to the Casbah. Karim would have been furious if you'd let them escape."

"They did escape," David drawled. "They came

back of their own volition when I assured them that Yusef's imprisonment was all a mistake."

"Some mistake," Billie said indignantly. "Holding an innocent man under arrest without charges is usually considered criminal."

"Not in an absolute monarchy like Sedikhan," Clancy said. "And he wasn't precisely under arrest. We were just detaining him until we could check out his story."

"For heaven's sake, you had all the information you could possibly need in my dossier," Billie said. "What else did you need to know?"

"The report touched only lightly on Ibraheim. When he burst in here insisting rather violently that he had to see you at once, we decided we'd better check more thoroughly into his background."

"Violently?" Billie asked.

"I think you could say that knocking out one of the gate guards and giving the other one a black eye could be termed violent."

"Oh, Yusef." Billie sighed, turning to the scowling giant next to her. "You didn't."

"They would not let me in," Yusef said. "A house with soldiers and rough guards is not a place for you. It is not safe. I was not there to protect you."

"But I was there," David said quietly. "I can understand how you might have been concerned, but from now on you'll know that Billie will always be safe when she's with me." His eyes held the other man's steadily. "Won't you, Yusef?"

Yusef's answering gaze was strangely searching before he nodded slowly. "Yes, Lisan, she will be safe with you."

"But will you be safe with her?" Karim Ben Raschid's voice cut through the silence of the people gathered in the foyer. He strode toward them, a barbarically splendid figure in the long crimson robe that covered his nightclothes. "A woman who has friends who wreak violence wherever they go, a woman who was able to hold two of my soldiers at gunpoint and free her accomplice."

"Accomplice!" Billie sputtered.

"Who could I be safer with?" David's eyes were twinkling. "I think from now on I'll just let her be my bodyguard. You should have seen her standing there with that rifle cradled in her arm like a guerrilla warrior. It was a brilliant coup, Karim. I would have thought an old border campaigner like you would have appreciated that fact."

Karim shot Billie a glance that for a brief moment mirrored a grudging admiration. "It was a well-executed raid," he admitted gruffly. "And she has a brave heart." His expression hardened. "But that doesn't mean it's a loyal or honorable heart. That is still to be proven."

"Find all the proof you want," David said. "But while you're doing it, both Billie and Yusef are to be free as birds. Yusef will have quarters near Billie, and you'll issue orders that their movements are to be totally unrestricted."

Karim muttered a brief expletive beneath his breath. "That sounds remarkably like an order, David." His eyes were blazing. "I am not a man who obeys when a boy commands. I will do what I think best."

"But I'm not a boy any longer," David said gently. "I think you sometimes forget that, Karim. I'm a man with a will of my own. It will only be a command if you refuse it as a request."

"And if I do?"

David's eyes were sad. "Then I'll say good-bye, old

friend." His voice was regretful. "And I don't want to do that. We've been through too much together."

Karim inhaled sharply; and suddenly, for the first time, he looked like the old man he was. "She means that much to you?"

David nodded silently.

It was a long, painful moment before Karim shrugged. "It will be as you wish. Guard yourself well, since you will not permit me to do it for you." He turned away. "It is late. I will see you at breakfast." He strode down the hall, his carriage as proud and indomitable as ever.

"My God, he backed down," Clancy muttered incredulously. "I've never seen him do that in all the years I've been working for him."

"And it hurt him to do it," David said, a glint of pain in his own eyes. "Defeat doesn't come easily to Karim." He drew a deep breath and turned to Clancy. "Why don't you find Yasmin and see if she can arrange Yusef's quarters? I think she should be in Billie's apartment. She was too worried to go to bed, so I told her to wait there." He smiled at Yusef. "If you'll go along with Clancy, I promise you that your accommodations will be considerably better than the last ones you occupied."

Yusef cast a hesitant look at Billie and then a more thoughtful one at David. He shrugged and followed Clancy swiftly down the corridor.

"What would you have done if he'd called your bluff?" Billie asked softly.

"Then I'd have left Zalandan," David said quietly. "I don't bluff, Billie, and I don't lie to old friends like Karim. He knew that or he wouldn't have backed down."

"You'd actually have left the Casbah?" Billie asked incredulously. "I can't believe it. You're really fond of that arrogant old dictator. It shows all over you."

"I love him," David said simply. "But I made you a promise and I had to keep it. You'd have gone away if I hadn't."

A warm, melting glow seemed to be passing through every atom of her being, leaving a soft radiance in its wake. "And would you have cared so much?"

"I think you know the answer to that." He smiled, and again there was that trace of sadness. "Or perhaps you don't want to know. I've tried to tell you since the beginning, but you won't believe me. Well, I'm going to say the words anyway, even though I know you're not ready to hear them. I love you, Billie Callahan, and I'd like to spend the rest of my life with you." He raised a hand as she opened her lips to speak. "But I'll take whatever you'll give me. What *will* you give me, Billie?"

A torrent of emotion was cascading through her in a confused stream. Panic, sadness, joy. They were all there, and all so powerful they were tearing her apart. He was standing there looking at her with those wise, sad eyes, and she wanted to say anything, do anything, he wanted. Did she love him? The answer came with a simple stunning force. Of course she loved him. And that knowledge was all the more frightening for the diligence with which she'd avoided accepting it.

No, she couldn't love him. It was infatuation. It would go away and then there'd be no danger. No danger of pain. But there was pain in David's eyes, and she couldn't bear it. She couldn't say the words he wanted to hear, but she had to do something to take that pain and sadness away. If she didn't, the aching agony she was feeling would kill her.

She moved a step closer and slipped into his arms. She could feel the waiting in him, and the tenseness. "David?" He was so warm and strong, so dear, Lisan. "I can't." The tears were running down her cheeks. "I think I do care for you. I don't know . . ."

His arms were around her in a firm, comforting embrace, and his voice was a soothing murmur in her ear. "It's all right, windflower. Easy. I knew it was too soon."

"David." Her voice was muffled against his chest. "You said you'd take whatever I'd give. Will you take . . . the blossoming?"

He stiffened against her. "Hell no," he said tersely. "I'm not about to pressure you into a commitment like that just because you're feeling guilty that you can't give me what I want."

"No." She pushed away from him so she could look into his eyes. "It's not that. I want to belong to you." And suddenly she knew every word was true. It wasn't pity, but a fierce desire to wrest something precious for herself to take with her when she left him. For she would leave him. She always had to leave when the fear came. "Please, I *want* it, David."

He was gazing at her searchingly, and gradually the tension was ebbing out of him. "I'd be a fool not to give you what you want, then, wouldn't I?" He touched her cheek gently with an index finger. "And I'm not a fool, sweetheart. So we'll have our blossoming tonight." His finger moved down to her lips and traced them lovingly. "But first I want you to think about it and make sure it's what you really want. I'll be in the greenhouse in an hour, and if you decide that it is, Yasmin will tell you how to get there." He suddenly pulled her close, and his lips were a hot, desperate brand that burned to the heart. "Oh, God, I hope you come, love."

Before she could answer he had pushed her away and was striding down the hall without a backward glance.

When she opened the door to the greenhouse, she couldn't believe the sight that met her eyes. The exterior had appeared very large as she approached it from the main residence, but she had no idea how enormous it was until she stepped inside. The glass roof loomed almost seventy-five feet above her, and the exquisite garden sheltered by the paneled arch was utterly breathtaking. It was as beautifully designed as any outdoor garden. Winding paths wandered through lush meadows of flowers and trees of every description. Moonlight streamed through the glass, capturing heart-catching beauty in mystic radiance. Persian lilacs, golden marigolds, scarlet geraniums, russet chrysanthemums standing proud, delicate white violets clustering cozily. And the scents! Dear heaven, the scents were so heady and intoxicating that she could only stand quite still for a moment and let the delicate fragrance of a thousand living blossoms drift over her in a mist of delight. She closed the door behind her, and it broke the stillness with a sharp click.

"Billie? Over here."

She followed David's voice with a dreamlike slowness down a path that led past oleander trees dripping with ivory blooms, jacarandas whose lilac flowers brushed her face like a velvet kiss, past a mosaic fountain brimming and overflowing with lacy ferns and starlike flowers instead of water. She was sure it had to be a dream, for nothing could be this bewitchingly lovely.

Until she made a turn in the path and saw David kneeling beside a plot of earth just ahead, the square, filigreed Moorish lantern on the ground beside him casting a mellow pool of light around him. He was dressed in somber black jeans and a black long-sleeved shirt that made the gold of his hair and the bronze of his skin seem even more vibrant in contrast. There was nothing dreamlike about David.

He turned as she paused a few yards away, and the brilliant smile that lit his face when he saw her was more beautiful than the loveliness of the garden. "I was afraid you'd changed your mind," he said quietly. "Come here beside me. I want to show you something."

She came forward slowly and sank down beside him. "Your garden is so lovely, David," she said, her voice throaty. "I've never dreamed anything could be so magical."

"It is magical, isn't it?" His eyes were intent on the tender green sprigs he was planting so carefully. "So much life and beauty in one place. Sometimes I can almost hear the growth and the rhythms."

"Rhythms?"

"There are rhythms all around us, if we stop to listen. Just as there are rhythms inside of all of us. Sometimes they're harsh and strained and sometimes clear and bell-like. Haven't you ever noticed?"

She shook her head. "I don't believe I ever have."

He took her hand in his and placed it on the rich, warm earth before them. "Feel," he said softly.

"Feel the life throbbing and the music singing from the darkness. Can you feel it, Billie?"

"Yes, I can feel it," she said in wonder.

With his strong hand covering hers and the warm earth caressing the palm of her hand, she *could* feel it. But she wasn't sure if it was the rhythm of the earth or David's vibrant life force she was feeling. Perhaps it was both. For in that moment David seemed to have a primitive affinity with all the facets of nature around him.

His hand tightened convulsively. Then he slowly released her. "I'm glad." He drew a deep breath. "I shouldn't have touched you—I'm wanting you too much right now. I have to finish this first." He grimaced ruefully. "I had these sprigs flown in, but I wasn't planning on putting them out until tomorrow. I needed something to take my mind off the waiting, so I started to plant them tonight."

"What are they?"

"Anemones," he answered. "Windflowers."

She laughed shakily. "I don't believe I've ever heard of a man postponing a seduction to plant flowers. I think perhaps I should be insulted, even if they are my namesake."

"Not a seduction, a blossoming." His hands were rapidly finishing his task. "And these aren't just flowers I'm planting. It's a sort of ritual. I believe in rituals, sweetheart. I think they make life more meaningful and beautiful."

"And what is this ritual?"

"Love," he said simply. "I'm planting my windflower in the center and surrounding her with pinks. That's one of the flowers that means love, you know."

A windflower surrounded by love. How incredibly moving. She felt her throat tighten with emotion.

"No, I didn't know. I thought only roses meant love."

"No, there are any number of flowers that have the same meaning." There was an odd flicker of pain in his face, and he lowered his eyes once more to his sprigs. "I planted an entire garden of love once. For my mother, at the ranch in Texas."

"What a wonderful thing to do," Billie said. "How she must have loved it."

"No, not wonderful. Necessary." His tone was weary. "I'd taken so much from her, and she couldn't accept what I wanted to give her." He paused, and there was a little thickness in his voice when he continued. "I thought perhaps it would be a way of easing her pain."

"Pain?"

"I nearly destroyed her as well as myself when I experimented with those drugs in college. Maybe I deserved it for being such a God-awful fool, but she didn't." He closed his eyes. "You can't imagine what those first years were like. The terrible nightmares, the fear. It was like being burned alive. And then, when I started to get well, I wasn't the same person I'd been before. It was as if that other David had been destroyed when I took acid in the dorm that night and I'd been born again from the flames of the hell I went through. She couldn't accept that new David. She nearly had a nervous breakdown, and my father thought for a while that he'd lost both of us."

He opened his eyes, and she felt a stabbing pain as she saw the weariness and sadness there. "So Bree and Alex took me away to Sedikhan and tried to bring back the son she'd known before that night. The doctors . . ." He shrugged. "They may have been able to restore my memory and my brainpower, but they couldn't perform miracles. They couldn't resurrect the man who had died in those flames. I thought it might be enough for her, but when I went back to the ranch for a visit two years ago, things hadn't really changed. She was still uneasy around me, still hurting inside. She's a very loving, caring person, and I'd killed the person she loved most in the world besides my father. She needed someone to love, but she couldn't love me." His hands clenched suddenly in the earth. "She couldn't love me any more."

"David . . ." Billie could scarcely see through the mist of tears. She could feel his pain as if it were her own, and it was almost unbearable. "Perhaps you were mistaken. She must have loved you." Who could help but love him?

"No, I wasn't mistaken. I'd hurt her too much, and I'm only a reminder of her pain now." His hands slowly unclenched, and the dark earth sifted through his fingers. "I've never been back since that visit. I met my father in New York last year when I had to fly over on some business about the book, but I haven't seen my mother. I don't know if I'll ever see her again." He drew a deep, shaky breath as he sat back on his heels. He reached for the towel beside him and began wiping his hands. "But she's going to be all right. She's happy now. I sent her someone she *could* love. A sweet, pretty child who needed love as much as she needed to give it."

Zilah. He'd found a way to heal everybody's hurt but his own. God, she wanted to heal that hurt. To hold him and find a way to banish the sadness that still lingered on his face.

He turned to look at her, and when he saw her face he smiled and shook his head. "Hey, don't look like that. There's nothing to be sad about. I told you, she's fine. And I'm all right too. I have friends who love me, and now Sedikhan is my home. We can't have everything."

But she wanted him to have everything, she thought fiercely. She wanted him to have beauty, love, and everything he'd ever wanted. He *deserved* it.

"No, we can't have everything." She smiled up at him a little mistily. "But we can try. If you remember, that's why I'm here."

"How could I forget?" He reached out and took her hand in his, his eyes suddenly twinkling. "After all, my anatomy has been very aggressively reminding me since I left you in the hall tonight." He picked up the towel and the lantern with one hand and, still holding her hand with the other, pulled her to her feet. "Come, milady, let me show you to your chamber."

He led her toward a tall flowering hedge that occupied a central position in the greenhouse, stopping only a moment to wash his hands at one of the mosaic fountains. Closer up she could see that the high, symmetrical wall of the hedge was broken by an arched opening. Then they were going through that opening and she found herself in the chamber he had promised her. Enclosed by hedges on three sides and a lattice wall of golden honeysuckle on the fourth, it was like a cozy little room. There was a wrought-iron bench on the far side of the enclosure, and in the center was a large mat covered in ivory silk that shimmered in the lantern light.

"I come here sometimes when I'm having trouble mapping out a chapter," David said, putting down the lantern on the mossy ground beside the silk-sheathed mat. "It's very pleasant and soothing."

She chuckled. "Those must be some sensual chapters if they're thought out on silk sheets."

"That's a new addition," he answered. "In your honor, windflower. You'll notice the sheets are ivory. I remember how you hated the idea of clashing." He turned her in his arms with a tenderness that caused the trembling to start deep inside her. "No clashing tonight, love. Just a sweet blending, a perfect joining." His lips caressed hers in a sensual brushing, tasting, teasing that made her open them with unconscious yearning. Then his tongue was plunging into her moist warmth and her lips closed hungrily on it, sucking and nibbling until she could feel the gentleness leave his arms as he crushed her to him with a low groan. His iron-hard arousal was pressed against her, and she welcomed it with an involuntary upward thrusting that made him give another gasping groan deep in his throat. It was odd what a savage satisfaction she received from that helpless cry of need. She rubbed slowly against him in deliberate provocation, reveling in the half gasps that shuddered through him at every movement. She wanted him to feel that need, wanted it to build up until it broke free and exploded into the same primitive desire she was having. There was a wild, aching throbbing between her thighs that was being stoked into liquid flame.

His hands suddenly clutched roughly at her buttocks, and he began a thrusting against her that caused her hands to grab at his shoulders and hang on desperately as she felt her knees melt and go weak. He lifted his head, and his face was flushed, his eyes dark and glazed. "That's another one of life's rhythms, Billie." He slowly rotated her against him while still thrusting. "Do you like that one?"

"Yes. Oh, yes." Her head was thrown back, her throat arched with the tension that was mounting at a pace that was burning her alive.

"I'll show you other rhythms that you'll enjoy even more." His hands were squeezing her in tempo with the thrusting of his lower body. "How much do you want me, sweetheart? Do you want me inside you as much as I want to be there? Tell me what you want me to do to you."

"I want you." She could barely speak as she felt the heat tingling through every vein of her body. He rotated her against him again, and she inhaled sharply as she felt a jab of desire so intense that she thought it would rip her apart. "Please, David. I want you there *now*."

His hips were still, and he was holding her pressed against him with urgent strength. She could feel his heart thundering against her and the harsh sound of his shallow breathing. Then he was pushing her away from him. "And heaven knows I want you now too," he said thickly. "But not yet, windflower. I want to make it as perfect as I can for both of us. I told you I believe in rituals. The blossoming is a very important one." His hand was unbuttoning her black tunic top and lifting it swiftly over her head. He threw it aside carelessly, his hot gaze on her small, uptilted breasts. "My tulips. I'm going to make them blossom, too, love." His hands were on the fastening of her khakis, and then he was pushing them, together with the minute bikini panties she wore, over her hips and down her legs. Falling to his knees, he carefully lifted her legs out of them, removing her sandals at the same time.

He sat back on his heels, and his glowing eyes ran over her lingeringly, in a way that was only a breath away from incendiary. "Beautiful, strong, and graceful." He leaned forward to nestle his head against her belly, the slight roughness of his cheek causing little shivers of heat to go through her. "And sexy. Definitely sexy, Billie."

"I'm not—"

"You are," he interrupted firmly. "Shall I show you how sexy?" He rubbed his head against her, his teeth nipping occasionally at the soft flesh, his tongue tasting her with an erotic delicacy. "It's responsiveness that makes a woman sexy, sweetheart. Let's see just how responsive you are." His fingers were running with sensual pleasure through the soft down that guarded the center of her womanhood. "You're trembling. I can feel the heat of you beneath my hands. So soft and yearning." He was stroking her, rubbing her with a circular motion that wrung a tiny moan from her. "Sexy," he whispered. "Completely and marvelously sexy." Then he was pulling her down on him, his arms going around her and his lips covering hers with a passion that took her breath away. He bore her back on the silk counterpane of the mat, covering her body with his own. She could feel the burning heat of him through his clothes.

"You're still dressed," she muttered as his lips left her own to wander down her throat in a hundred hot kisses.

"Yes." He lifted his head, his eyes oddly smoky as they met hers. "And you're completely naked. How does that make you feel?"

"What?" she asked confusedly. "I don't know. Vulnerable, I guess."

"Nothing else?" he asked softly. As he rubbed his chest against hers, the crisp cotton of his shirt caused a slight friction that made her tense. "Isn't there something else, too, love?"

Yes, there was something else. The vulnerability of her own nakedness, the dominance of his still-clothed body, were engendering an erotic excitement that was bringing a hot flush to every inch of her exposed form. She buried her face in his shoulder with a low cry, her back arching up to meet him.

"I thought so." His voice was hoarse as he parted her legs with one of his. "I think I'll just wait awhile to undress." His lips were moving over the rise of her breast. "It's time I tasted your honey, Billie." His hand cupped her breast, and his head bent slowly to the pink rosette that was offering itself eagerly to his mouth. "Let me suckle at your pretty breasts." His mouth closed on her with a dainty sipping and then suddenly changed to a strong suction as his hand closed and opened around her breast in a gentle milking pressure that caused her head to thrash feverishly back and forth on the silk counterpane.

"Rhythms, Billie," he murmured as his mouth continued the tempo that was turning her into an aching void wanting to be filled. "Rhythms."

Then he suddenly drew his knee up between her thighs until it was resting against the center of her being. She gasped as he began to rub back and forth against her. The rough denim of his jeans was a hot abrasion causing flashes of sensation that were beginning to shake her apart. Rhythms, she thought hazily, the rhythm of her pounding heart, the rhythm of his lips against her breast, the rhythm of his knee against the sensitive core of her. Hot, mind-exploding rhythms.

David was breathing as if his lungs were starved for oxygen when he finally lifted his head and gazed into her flushed and languorous face. "I don't think I can wait much longer. I think we'd better move to some of the other rhythms, love."

He rolled off her and stood up, gazing down at her with a face that was heavy with sensuality. He unbuttoned his black shirt with hands that trembled slightly. "In a moment I'll be just as vulnerable as you." He grinned ruefully. "If I can stop my hands from shaking enough to get these damn buttons undone." He pulled the shirt out of his pants and shrugged out of it, his bronze shoulders taking on a copper luster in the flickering lantern light. "I think we've got it made, windflower."

It appeared that he had, for in an amazingly short time he was stripped completely and was dropping down on the mat beside her. "Come here, love. I want to see how well we flow together." He pulled her to him and strained her so close, she felt as if she were being absorbed into him. His sleek, warm flesh, the slight roughness of the hair on his chest, the hardness of the muscles of his thighs, it was all terribly arousing. For him, too, it seemed, for she could feel that arousal prodding demandingly against her. She unconsciously nestled her hips closer, and she heard his low, husky laugh beneath her ear. "Trying to strike up an acquaintance? I assure you, you're going to be on exceptionally good terms very soon." He pushed her away, turning her over on her back. He parted her legs and slid lithely between them. He sat back on his heels and looked down at her a long moment, his sapphire eyes darkened to almost navy. "Lord, that's wonderful. Ready and waiting and so lovely." He edged closer, so that the warm velvet length of him was pressing against her.

She gave a little gasp, and she could feel something clench inside her. He was rubbing against her now as his knee had before, and it was sending little electric shocks to every nerve in her body. His face was very intent, and she could see his chest move with the labored force of his breathing. His fingers were stroking her now, preparing her, and she writhed against them helplessly, feeling as if every inch of her were on fire. Then his hands were gone and he was pressing against her once more, this time with a more urgent, not a teasing, pressure.

"David," she said, her eyes wild and feverish in her flushed face. "I've never—"

"I know," he interrupted gently. "I think I know everything about you, love. I've learned you by heart."

Then he was entering her with painstaking care. So large. So full. Joined. How wonderful to be part of him. Even though she was aching with frustration for more, this was beautiful too.

He paused, his eyes narrowed in concern. "A little pain now, windflower. But with growth there's always a bit of pain, and what comes afterward is the blossoming. And that's a miracle." He leaned over, and his lips took hers with a tenderness so intense, she felt her heart stop.

He thrust forward forcefully, smothering her little cry with his lips. He gave her an instant to become accustomed to him. Then he was moving, plunging, thrusting, with gradually increasing force. It was fire and need and an emptiness that at last was being filled. She arched upward and began to meet his rhythm with her own.

Rhythm. Yes, another one, the most powerful one of all. Somewhere outside herself she could feel the rhythm of their bodies merging with the silent throbbing tempo of everything about them. The rich earth. The flowering shrubbery, the silver moonlight streaming in and bathing them in its mystical glow. Everything.

Then he was thrusting even harder, lifting her hips to bring her closer, him deeper. She could feel the tension mounting within them both like a tightly closed bud that was growing impatient to unfold and unite with the sunlight. Then the bud burst into glory, rapture, beauty, reaching up to meet the warmth of the sun. The sun, David. The blossoming, oh, dear heavens, the blossoming!

"A miracle." His murmur in her ear was a mere breath, his heart still pounding erratically. "I told you it would be a miracle, windflower." He rolled over on his side, keeping her with him. "A miracle of joy. It always will be with us."

It was strange, but she could still feel the warmth of that miracle of the blossoming even as her heart-beat slowed and steadied. She was still wrapped in its loving sunlight. "It was unbelievable."

"Believe it," he said thickly, his arms tightening around her. "Because it's going to happen again. We can make it happen. Aren't we lucky, love?"

"Yes, so lucky," she murmured drowsily. "Can we do it again soon?"

"Very soon, love. As soon as you've taken a little nap. You've had a hell of a day, and I think you deserve a little rest."

Day. It had been only one day, she realized with surprise. So many things had happened in that short space of time. Her lovely guitar, Yusef, the Silver Crescent. They all seemed as if they'd taken place in another century. Nothing was real but this moment in David's arms. "Are you sure it's not you who needs the rest?" she drawled, nibbling teasingly at his shoulder. "After all, it's not many men who could withstand the temptation of a sexy wench like me."

"Sexy?"

She nodded, her hands tangling in the soft mat of the hair on his chest. "Sexy. You've convinced me. If response equals sexuality, then I'm the randiest sex goddess on record." She lifted her head to meet his lips in a long, sweet kiss. "See how I respond to you, David?"

"Oh, yes, love." His voice was throaty as one hand stroked her hair back from her face with gossamer gentleness. "Just as I respond to you. And I always will. Fifty years from now I'll still want you if you do nothing more than smile at me or wrinkle your nose."

She stiffened against him as she felt a little frisson of uneasiness. "That's a long time," she said, trying to keep her voice light. "I think I told you how I felt about forever."

His hand was still, and then continued its soothing stroking. "Don't panic, love. I'm not trying to tie you down, as much as I'd like to. Stay with me as long as you can. That's all I ask."

She nestled closer, her heart aching with love. Oh, God, it *was* love. If it were mere infatuation, how could it invade every bit of her heart and mind? "It's not that I don't want to stay," she whispered haltingly. "It's just that I can't. Never. I think that I'm happy, that I've found a place to call home, and then something happens. I get frightened and panic. I have to run away." She laughed shakily. "Crazy, huh?"

"No, it's not crazy." His lips brushed her temple. "Don't worry. I understand, windflower. I know you by heart, remember?"

By heart. Yes, she knew him by heart too. That was the only way to know David. "I'll try," she promised gravely. "I'll try to stay, David."

"That's all I want," David said simply. "We'll take what we can and fill every moment with laughter and miracles. Now close your eyes, sweetheart. I want to hold you in my arms and watch you sleep."

Her lids slowly closed, but it was as much to hide their moist brightness as to tempt slumber. She didn't go to sleep for some time as she lay in his arms and thought wistfully about the laughter and the miracles.

Seven

"Hold still, Yusef. It will only be a minute and I'll have you under the dryer." She snapped the last of the curling rods shut and stood back to appraise the rows of tiny rods marching down Yusef's head. "That should do it," she said as she secured a plastic bag over his hair.

"My God, Billie, what are you doing?" David's face was blank with astonishment as he stood in the doorway of her room.

"What?" she asked as she swung the already roaring hood of the dryer over Yusef's head. "Oh, hi, David. I'll be through here in just a second." She yelled to Yusef over the noise of the dryer. "Eight minutes." He gave a glum nod and closed his eyes with a long-suffering expression.

Billie was frowning crossly as she turned and walked toward David. "You'd think I was sticking him with knives. What a baby!"

"Billie, would it be too much to ask *what* he's

being a baby about?" He closed the door and leaned against it, his bewildered gaze on the giant under the hair dryer.

"I'm giving him a permanent, but he's being most uncooperative. He's complained about everything from the stink of the waving lotion to the amount of time it took me to roll it." She scowled. "It's not as if I'm a professional hairdresser. Of course it took me a little time." She sniffed her fingers and made a face. "He's right about the waving lotion, though."

"A permanent," David echoed blankly. "Why are you giving him a permanent?"

"Because I want him to look like Tony Geary, that actor who was on *General Hospital.*"

"General Hospital?"

"It's a soap opera. I got hooked on it for a while when I was working at the Office of Indian Affairs at the reservation of the Rainbow people."

David shook his head. "I'm not even going to ask who the Rainbow people are. I'm too confused already. Let's just stick to Yusef. Why do you want him to look like a TV actor, for heaven's sake?"

"Not *any* TV actor. Tony Geary," Billie said patiently. "It's very important he look like Luke and not Robert or Allen or any of the others. Luke is sensitive, even a little vulnerable. The others appear to be much stronger." Her brow wrinkled thoughtfully. "Not that Luke isn't strong, it's just—"

He put his hand over her lips. "Let me catch up. I thought you wanted him to look like Tony Geary. Now we're switching to Luke. Which one are we cloning?"

She kissed his hand absently before pulling it

away. "Tony Geary is the actor who plays Luke Spencer. They're one and the same."

"That's a relief—I thought we were getting mixed up." His lips twitched. "Now everything is perfectly clear. Luke's the sensitive one?"

"Right, that's very important," Billie said earnestly. "We don't want him to look sleek or sophisticated or anything like that. We're going for sensitive and vulnerable."

"That's very intelligent of us," he said solemnly, his eyes dancing. "And a permanent is going to make Yusef sensitive?"

"Yusef *is* sensitive," Billie said a little indignantly. "He's a very caring person. I'm just trying to make him look that way."

"I wouldn't think of insulting your little lamb," David said soothingly, glancing at the fierce Hercules imprisoned under the hair dryer. "I don't think there's a man in Sedikhan who would."

"That's the whole point. Everyone is afraid of him because he seems so terrifying. They don't bother to look beyond the facade and see how gentle he is."

Gentle. David had a sudden memory of the gate guards who'd been trampled and crushed by that "gentle" giant only two weeks ago. "How very unperceptive of them. And you've found the solution?"

"Curls!" She beamed. "Luke has curls. Lots of them, all over his head. They have a sort of frizzy softness. Who could be afraid of a man with a mop like Shirley Temple?"

"He's going to look like Shirley Temple?" David shook his head. "Somehow I don't think so."

"Of course not. I told you I was aiming for Tony Geary. Manly, but sensitive."

"I'm glad you opted for the manly. I don't think Yusef would appreciate looking like Shirley Temple," he said dryly. "I'm surprised he's letting himself be coerced into this beauty treatment."

"Well, he's not doing it with very good grace," she said with a disgruntled glance at the still-scowling Yusef. "I don't think he'd let me do it all except for Daina."

"Daina? Who's Daina? Another soap-opera character?"

Billie shook her head. "She and her family run that jewelry stall in the bazaar. She's a pretty little thing, but very timid. She's scared to death of Yusef. I met her yesterday morning when I strolled down there with him." She made a face. "Since you were so involved with your writing, you couldn't honor me with your presence until after lunch."

"You're the one who insisted I stay at the Casbah," he protested. "You said you had some personal shopping you wanted to do." His sapphire eyes were glowing softly. "I think I've demonstrated that you're my primary occupation these days. The book could have waited."

She dropped her gaze to the front of his shirt, feeling the familiar warmth surge through her. "You've been spending too much time with me," she said, a little gruffly. "I was there when you got that phone call from your editor, remember? You promised him you'd send off the finished manuscript at the end of the week. I know you're working on it in the evenings, but if I didn't take up so much of your time during the day, you wouldn't have to work so late. You didn't come to bed until almost three last night. I don't like you to work that hard."

He touched her cheek with a teasing finger. "It

doesn't seem to exhaust me to the point of no return." His eyes were twinkling. "I still woke you up and managed to while away another hour or so. Didn't I display a sufficient degree of energy for you?"

A little tingle started in the pit of her stomach as she remembered just how that energy had been directed. "Oh, you were adequate," she said airily, gazing up at him impishly from beneath her lashes. "Of course, I've seen you show greater stamina. You went right to sleep after only the second time. I was beginning to think you didn't think I was sexy any more."

"Oh, I find you sexy," he said softly, a little flame beginning to light in the depths of his eyes. "You were gone when I woke up, or I would have proved that to your complete satisfaction. That's why I came looking for you. Why don't you come to my room and I'll demonstrate it right now?"

She took an impulsive step forward and then stopped and shook her head. "I've got to finish Yusef's permanent." She sighed. "I want him to be in top shape when he goes to see Daina this afternoon."

"Oh, yes, the timid Daina. I hope she appreciates the sacrifices we're all making for her sake. Was all this really necessary?"

"Oh, yes. Yusef is positively besotted with her, and she's absolutely terrified of him," Billie said seriously. "He won't be nearly so intimidating without all that wild hair. She'll see him through entirely new eyes."

"Tony Geary?"

She nodded happily, and he tried to smother his grin as he leaned forward and gave her a light kiss on the tip of her nose. "Then, I guess I'm banished to my desk for the next few hours. You're not going to give him a beauty mask and a manicure as well?"

"This isn't all that amusing. Men do have permanents, these days, just like women, you know." She suddenly grinned. "And you shouldn't talk. That braid you were wearing in your portrait wasn't exactly macho."

"Touché," he said. "Hoisted with my own petard."

There was a perfunctory knock on the door behind him and Clancy entered without waiting for an invitation. "Yasmin said you were here, David. I have to speak to you for a moment." He nodded at Billie. "Hello, Billie. Sorry about bursting in here like this." His full attention was given again to David as he pulled an envelope out of the back pocket of his cords. "I think you'd better take a look at this."

David took the envelope and slipped the note from it. He perused it casually, his expression impassive. "Nothing to get upset about," he said, handing the note and envelope back to Clancy. "Perhaps a little more explicit than usual, but no different from the rest."

"The difference lies in the fact that this one wasn't in the mail, but slipped under the front door of the Casbah," Clancy said grimly. "With two gate guards and two at the front entrance, that *couldn't* have happened. But it did. Which means Ladram has either managed to assume a good guise to penetrate the gates or he's bribed someone to do his errands for him. Either way it means he's coming closer. He's probably here in the city and wants you to know it."

"Good," David said. "Then we'll be through with

him soon." He nodded toward the note in Clancy's hand. "Judging by that, he's getting very impatient. He's positively salivating."

How could he be so casual? Billie wondered with a shiver. Just thinking of Ladram in the same city and ready to pounce on David filled her with cold terror. "May I see the note?" she asked through stiff lips.

David cast a narrowed glance at her set, pale face and shook his head. "I don't think so, Billie. It's a little ugly."

"So is Ladram," Clancy said tersely. "And I agree that it's just as well that everything's coming to a head, but it also means the danger is doubled. For God's sake be careful, David."

"Always," David said lightly.

Clancy snorted. "Almost never," he corrected gloomily, shaking his head in disgust. Suddenly his glance fell upon Yusef, across the room, and his eyes widened. "Good Lord, what on earth are you doing to him?"

"It's not some futuristic torture implement." David's eyes were suddenly dancing. "And the look of pain on his face isn't physical, but mental. Billie's giving him a permanent."

"A permanent?" Clancy responded dazedly, his eyes on the scowling face of the man beneath the hair dryer. "Yusef?"

"Oh, my goodness, it's time he came out," Billie said frantically. "He'll get too much curl!" She was running across the room to the dryer.

"Curl?" Clancy's voice was choked, his eyes bright. "Oh, Lord, I can't stand it. I want to laugh but I'm afraid that ferocious behemoth will annihilate me. Curls!"

"But not Shirley Temple," David said solemnly.

"Billie assured me that wouldn't do at all. Frizzy, soft, sensitive curls."

"Dear heaven, don't go on." Clancy's shoulders were shaking with silent laughter. "I can't stand it. I don't even want to know why she's doing it. It would be too much."

"I wouldn't think of confiding Yusef's personal affairs," David said righteously. "I'm every bit as sensitive as Luke Spencer"—he touched a lock of his hair—"though my coiffure doesn't reflect it." His eyes widened in mock alarm. "You don't think Billie will want to change it."

"Damn you, David." Clancy was heroically trying to keep a straight face. "Will you stop that? It would serve you right if she did. And there's every chance she just might. I've discovered Billie's almost immovable when she gets a bee in her bonnet. Karim wasn't all that pleased about her interference with the guards. I think he believed she was trying to ingratiate herself with an eye to subverting their loyalty."

"Interference with the guards?" David's eyes were suddenly narrowed with concern. "What the hell are you talking about? I haven't heard anything about that."

"She probably didn't think it was important. You know that cool night last week? She sent out one of the servants with a pitcher of hot spiced cider for the exterior guards and left orders that the same thing be done every evening. She said it was 'sinfully' inconsiderate to let the poor men shiver out there alone without something warm to comfort them."

David's lips curved in a tender smile as his eyes followed Billie's movements while she carefully unrolled the rods in Yusef's hair, her brow knotted in concentration. "That sounds like Billie." Suddenly the smile vanished. "She's been going outside the Casbah without me lately. Put a guard on her, Clancy. But for heaven's sake, don't let her know. She'd raise hell if she thought I was doubting she could take care of herself."

"Ladram?"

David nodded. "There's a slight possibility she might be a target, if he's as well-informed as you seem to think. I won't take the chance."

"I wish you'd be as careful with your own neck," Clancy said wryly as he turned to leave. "Are you going to stay and see Yusef's final unveiling or will you join me for a cup of coffee?"

"I'll go with you." David cast a last wistful glance at Billie. "She probably won't be finished for hours. Making Yusef vulnerable-looking sounds like a *long* project."

Clancy looked at Billie just as she was testing the springiness of one coarse curl while Yusef stared up at her with a wild-eyed, helpless expression. "I can see how long-term it could be." He gasped. "Lord, I've got to get out of here." He bolted out of the room. There was an amused grin on David's face as he followed more slowly.

The cotton gown was really very attractive, Billie thought with a little surge of pleasure. It didn't equal the haute-couture elegance of the dress she'd borrowed that first evening, of course. She'd bought this one in the bazaar for a ridiculously low price, but its cobalt-blue-and-black stripes contrasted nicely with her copper hair. The boat neck and empire waist gave her bosom a little oomph too. She certainly needed all the help she could get in that area.

"Sit down. I will do your hair," Yasmin said briskly as she entered the dressing room. "We must take special care to make you presentable this evening." She pushed Billie down on the vanity bench. "You can see how womanly and lovely you can look if you try. Sheikh Karim will be very pleased."

"Because of the gown?" Billie shook her head. "He's not that easy to please. Besides, I didn't do it for him. I just thought it would be a nice change."

Yasmin raised a skeptical eyebrow. "It is a change that will meet with his approval. Now, sit still and I will finish the task."

"Just a minute. I might as well listen to last night's tape while you're doing it. I want to see if there's anything worth keeping." She reached over to switch on the tape recorder on the vanity, and immediately the sound of her own soft voice filled the room.

"You sing very well," Yasmin said as she began to brush Billie's hair vigorously.

"Not really. I can carry a tune, and that's about it. But I do get a kick out of making up songs."

"Sheikh Karim likes your singing," Yasmin insisted. "I heard Mr. Donahue tell Lisan that he'd found your voice very pleasant when you sang for them in the library that evening."

"It must have hurt him to admit it." She shrugged. "Not that it matters. I only sang because David asked me to."

Yasmin fell silent, concentrating on her artistry, and Billie tried to focus her attention on the song she'd composed last night while David was busy at the typewriter. It wasn't bad. Not as good as the one she'd created the night before, but still not bad at all. She'd probably keep it. She was gathering quite a collection of "keeper" tapes these days, she realized with some surprise.

When David had talked her into taping the sessions she spent in his room playing and composing, she'd been very reluctant. She'd thought she would end up immediately taping over ninety percent of the tapes, and told him so.

"Try it," he'd coaxed. "It's a crime to waste any creative effort. How many songs have you composed over the years and forgotten later? Keep a record so they'll always be with you."

So she'd tried it—and, to her surprise, found she liked the idea of creating something permanent, even if it was only an audio tape. Strange . . . when she'd never wanted anything resembling permanence in her life before. But then, these entire two weeks seemed to have no connection with her former life. It was as if she were suspended within a golden cloud, floating only over the present. And the present was so enchanting that she wanted to stay forever. Forever? No, she wasn't going to think about that. She was only going to take one day at a time and live in the sunlight with David. Maybe it *would* go on forever if she didn't think about it and could keep the fear at bay.

"I like that song. It's the best thing you've done yet," David said from where he stood in the doorway of the dressing room. He always looked so gorgeous in evening dress, she thought dreamily.

She reached for the switch of the tape recorder. "Thanks a lot," she said, making a face at him. "But that's not one of mine. I got tired of composing and started singing one of Carly Simon's songs."

"Oops!" His eyes were dancing. "Well, maybe

next week, windflower. You're getting better all the time."

Yasmin put down the comb and stood back. "You have not told Billie how nice she looks," she told David. "How lovely and *womanly*."

"Yasmin hates my jeans." Billie chuckled. "She's sure there's something unnatural about me."

"I could tell her different," David murmured. "There's no one more delightfully natural than you, love."

"Lisan," Yasmin demanded sternly.

"Yes, Yasmin, I was coming to that," David said. "Billie, may I see how lovely and particularly *womanly* you look this evening?" He raised an inquiring brow at Yasmin. "How's that, Yasmin?"

"Very poor, Lisan." Yasmin was gliding majestically past him to the door. "You must do better next time. She may never wear a dress again if you do not."

As she left the room, he murmured, "A state much to be desired. Especially if we also banish jeans and shirts and—"

"Shut up," Billie said, and laughed. "Yasmin wouldn't agree that was womanly, merely sluttish." She stood up. "Come on, we're going to be late for dinner. We don't dine that often with Karim, and we don't want to be rude."

"Don't we?" David asked teasingly. "I've been noticing a distinct softening in your attitude toward Karim lately. Could it be you're reconsidering your opinion of him? Let's see—what did you call him? Oh, yes, 'arrogant old dictator,' wasn't it?"

"Among other things," she said as she preceded him through the curtain into the bedchamber. "And all quite true." She glanced over her shoulder. "I just discovered that he's also very fair, has a rather wry sense of humor, and is more vulnerable than I thought. It's hard to dislike a man like that." She turned to pick up her evening bag from the bed and suddenly stopped short. "My guitar!"

Honorable Patches. Would she ever think of it in any other way now? It was lying on the end of the bed, and she slowly crossed the room to look down at it. The structural damage had been repaired with such skill that the cracks were hard to see, and it had been polished to a high gloss. But every single scratch and dent was still on its surface.

"It came in on the helicopter this afternoon," David said from behind her. "I would have given it to you then, but you didn't come to my room after you finished with Yusef."

"You had work to do," she said as she picked up the guitar and cradled it lovingly. "And I wanted to go to the bazaar with Yusef to see Daina's reaction to his new look."

"Was she impressed?"

Billie nodded. "I think so. At least she said a few words to him. Yusef was happy, anyway." Her fingers gently traced the scratches. "We'll just have to see how it goes."

David was beside her now. "You still like it best, don't you?" he asked. "I was hoping you'd grown used to the new one."

Her eyes flew to meet his. "Oh, I have. I love it." She smiled. "But you always give a warmer greeting to old friends when they've been away for a while. I'll get to feel the same way about the new one, given time." She put the guitar down on the bed. "I'll have to find a very special place for it."

"You already have." He reached out a hand and placed it over her heart. "You already have, love."

"I guess so." Her hand covered his and squeezed it. "Now we'd better get out of here."

"In a minute," he said, drawing her into his arms. "Let me hold you for a minute. It's been so long, I've forgotten how good you feel cuddled close like this."

She leaned against him, loving the warm, hard feel of him. "It hasn't been that long—just a few hours." But it seemed a long time to her too. She didn't feel complete without him any more.

"Long enough." He covered her lips in a long, sweet kiss that lit a glowing torch within her. "Too long." His hands came up to cup her breasts through the material of her gown. "I think I like you best in jeans and shirts. At least I can unbutton them and get to you. I have an idea this could be a very frustrating evening."

"Not womanly enough?" Billie asked impishly.

"Not sexy enough," David said. "You're always womanly. I just like to appreciate your more sensual attributes on occasion."

"On occasion," Billie repeated dryly.

"Well, morning, afternoon, and night," David said. "They're all occasions." He turned her toward the door. "I guess you're right. We'd better get out of this bedroom or I'm likely to elaborate on the subject, complete with demonstrations." He opened the door and glanced down to wink mischievously at her. "Besides, the sooner we can get dinner and the amenities over, the sooner I can whisk you back to my lair for fun and games."

"No miracles?" she asked with a grin.

"That goes without saying. Always miracles, love."

Eight

"Shareen!"

David's voice was no more astounded than his face as he released Billie's hand to accept the superbly manicured one of the woman who floated across the drawing room to him as soon as they entered.

She was one of the most gorgeous women Billie had ever seen. Raven-black hair gleamed against the creamy mat complexion, and the immense dark eyes that dominated her face were truly magnificent. Intelligent, warm, seductive, she was all of those things. Not to mention voluptuous. But she'd known that before, Billie thought numbly.

Then David was turning and introducing Shareen Nazare to her and that charming, intelligent smile was given to her. Billie heard herself reply politely, and it was a wonder she was coherent at all. Her throat had closed up, and she felt as if she could scarcely breathe. The pain was so sudden and so sharp it was like the thrust of a knife; panic bubbled higher in her every second.

She could hear the other woman murmuring something, those gorgeous eyes dancing with amusement, but she couldn't make any sense of it. She had to get out.

"Excuse me," she interrupted jerkily. "I'm suddenly not feeling well." Oh, God, that was the truth. "You'll have to forgive me."

She was vaguely conscious of Karim's and Clancy's expressions of surprise before she turned. She ran from the room and down the corridor as if she had wings. She heard David call out behind her, but she couldn't stop. She had to get away from that suffocating fear she'd known when she'd seen the woman smiling at David so intimately.

She'd barely slammed the door to her room when David burst through it. His face was pale, and there was concern, not anger, on his face. "For God's sake, what's wrong, Billie? You're white as a sheet. I've never seen you act like that before."

Why had she expected him to know what was wrong? He couldn't read her mind, only her heart. "I told you I sometimes do crazy things," she said feverishly. "I'm sorry I wasn't polite to your guest. You'll have to apologize to her for me." She sat down on the bed, her hands reaching automatically for the guitar she'd set there such a short time ago. It seemed like a decade. She cradled it against her, taking comfort from it. "She'll understand. She seemed quite pleasant."

"Shareen? Is that what all this is about?" There was a flicker of relief in his eyes. "Look, I told you, sweetheart, there was nothing there. She's certainly not here for my benefit. I knew Karim had sent for a *kadine* for himself, but I didn't know it would be Shareen. I guess I should have. She's very intelligent, and he appreciates that in his women."

"She's Karim's *kadine*?" Billie asked lifelessly. "Isn't he a little old for her?"

"You're never too old for an accomplished lady like Shareen," David said wryly. "She'll make him a very happy man tonight."

But she would rather have had David. Anyone would rather have David. "I'm sure she will."

"So there's no reason to be jealous or upset," David said gently. "You're the only important woman in my world."

For now. But how long could that last with a man like David? He wasn't only physically beautiful, he was beautiful inside too. He drew people like a magnet, and there were so many intelligent, lovely women out there in the world who would want him.

"I wasn't exactly jealous," she said, not looking at him. If there had been an element of jealousy in her feelings, it had been lost in the panic and the pain. In that moment she'd realized just how much she did love David Bradford, and it frightened her more than anything ever had in her whole life. It seemed to encompass her entire being, and it was growing stronger with every breath she took, with every moment she spent with him. "It's just that I suddenly felt again that I was that scrawny seven-year-old I once told you about. I could almost feel the orange braids sprouting." She laughed shakily. "That would have been pretty funny, wouldn't it?"

"It's not funny at all." Suddenly he was beside her. "Would you please stop hugging your old friend and hold me instead? I need you more, love."

She put the guitar aside and practically leaped

into his arms, clutching at him with a desperation that took his breath away. "I need you too," she said, burrowing her face into his shirt front. "I need you so much, David. Hold me. Please hold me."

"I'm holding you," David said thickly. "I'm holding you, windflower. I'll never let go."

He would someday. Love always went away from her. He'd be kind about it. He'd try to ease her desolation. He'd even be hurt himself when he found he couldn't do that. But it would be too late then.

"Billie." David's voice was an urgent murmur. "Talk to me. Let it out. I can't help you if you don't tell me what you're feeling. Can't you see it's tearing me apart to see you like this?"

"I don't want to talk." Her arms tightened around him. "I just want you to hold me. No, I want something else as well. I want you to make love to me. Will you do that?"

David's sapphire eyes were troubled. "I think we should talk first, love. I think you need that more."

Her trembling hands were at the buttons of his white dress shirt. "You're wrong. We can talk tomorrow." There was nothing she could talk about. Nothing she could say to him. "This is what I need tonight." She parted his shirt and laid her face against the soft thatch of hair on his chest. The strong cadence of his heart was beneath her ear. "Please, David."

"If that's what you really want." His hands were at the fastening at the back of her cotton gown and his voice was honey-dark. "That's all I ever want to do, love—give you what you need to have. What you want."

When their clothes were discarded and he would have borne her back on the amber silken sheets, she stopped him. "No, not yet. I want to look at you." She knelt on the bed, tugging at his hand, until he knelt facing her. "You're so beautiful. I used to think that men who were beautiful couldn't be virile-looking. But you are." Her gaze ran lovingly over broad golden shoulders that tapered to a hard, muscular waist and stomach. One hand ran caressingly over the tight firmness of his buttocks, and she felt him tense involuntarily. Her hand wandered around to clasp him with infinite tenderness. "You are—"

He jerked against her fondling hand. "It's nice to be appreciated, but you're teasing the hell out of me, sweetheart." He reached out to touch her cheek with gossamer gentleness. "I'd like to prove that virility when you're ready."

"Soon," she said, her eyes glowing almost feverishly. Her hand ran exploringly over the velvet hardness of him before leaving to rove over his stomach and up to the thatch of hair on his chest. "I want to memorize you. I want to know you so well that if I suddenly went blind, I'd still be able to see you before me. Would that be all right, David?"

There was a troubled little flicker in the depths of his eyes before he nodded slowly. "Will it help you, love?"

She nodded, her copper hair a bright curtain falling forward to shadow her face. "I think so."

"Then, I'm at your disposal," he said lightly. "Do with me what you will, *mon capitaine.*" He smiled. "And I promise you I'll enjoy every minute of it."

"I hope you will," she whispered. "I want that very much, David." She wanted to bring him an overflowing cornucopia of pleasure. She wanted to give him everything. Everything.

She pushed him gently back into a reclining

position on the bed and knelt over him. Her lips began a burning odyssey over his shoulders, down the whipcord muscles of his chest, to his stomach. They paused there a long, long time while she nibbled delicately, caressed with a teasing tongue, and then just lay there with her head on his stomach, her warm breath an erotic titillation of its own. Her hands began a lazy, teasing foray over the slightly rough hair that surrounded the root of his manhood, to the muscular column of his thighs. He was so strong, so golden, so completely and beautifully male.

His body was now a rigid wall of muscle. She could feel the painfully knotted tendons of his stomach beneath her cheek. His breath was coming in little shuddering gasps. As her lips followed the path of her hand, he gave a low groan, and his hips bucked upward. "Billie," he gasped, his sapphire eyes glazed. "It hurts. I want you so much it *hurts.*"

"I know. I know," she whispered gently, and her lips moved lovingly to soothe that hurt. He cried out, and his body convulsed with pleasure. She felt a deep rush of primitive satisfaction that she could give him that joy. He gave so much to everyone around him, he should have all the joy life could bring him.

Then, with a low cry, he reached down and pulled her up and over on her back. He was covering her body with his own the way he had in the sandstorm. He'd been so kind that day, protecting her, banishing her fears and pain. How she wished he could banish her pain now.

He was parting her thighs, and she welcomed him, leading him to her. Then he was within her, filling her, making her a part of him. He drew a deep breath and leaned forward to rest his head upon her breasts. Such a sweet, heavy weight. In the carpet shop he'd felt like that, nestling against her so lovingly. Shut out the memories, push them away. Think only of this moment.

He was trying to steady his breathing, his heart beating erratically against her. "You're not ready for me," he said shakily. "I can feel it. Give me a minute and I'll make it good for you."

"No, I'm ready for you," she said quickly. "It will be fine." She started a gentle undulating movement that caused a shudder to ripple through him. "Go ahead. I want you to."

"No." His hand moved down to the heart of her and began a gentle rotating that caused a deep clenching and opening within her. "I want you with me all the way."

He was being too careful, too tender. She could feel the panic exploding within her as she experienced again that loving kindness that was so much a part of him. He wouldn't take without giving, and she couldn't bear it if he gave to her right now. He mustn't make her love him any more. She loved him too much already.

She laughed with an effort. "I told you I was ready for you. Why won't you listen to me?" Her eyes were shining with a restless flame. "I guess I'll just have to show you."

She could feel him trying to temper his passion, to hold back, but she wouldn't let him. She knew the ways to pleasure him and fan the flame to white-hot, and she used them all. She didn't want him gentle and caring tonight. She wanted him hard and fast and almost brutal from his own need. In the end she had her way, and the force of his savage thrusts took her breath away. It was wild and hot and world-shaking, and when it was over they were both trembling.

"Did I hurt you?" David's eyes were concerned as he looked down at her. His chest was laboring with the force of his breathing. "I didn't mean to be that rough. God, I'm sorry, Billie."

"You gave me what I wanted," she said, her breathing as shallow as his own. She felt a slight soreness between her thighs and she knew she'd have a few bruises tomorrow. "It didn't matter."

"It matters very much," David said, a trace of grimness in his voice. "*Why* did you want it that way?"

"I don't want to talk about it now." She nestled close to him and determinedly closed her eyes. "I'm too sleepy."

"Billie." She heard the troubled frustration in his voice, but she didn't open her eyes. Then she heard him sigh resignedly and settle down beside her, drawing her closer. "Okay. Sleep, Billie, but tomorrow we talk."

She didn't answer, fighting the tears that were trying to slip from beneath her lashes. They wouldn't talk tomorrow. How could she tell him she loved him so much that she was afraid of the feeling's growing any greater? It was a thousand times worse than those other times now. What would it be like in six months or a year? She had to get away while she could still survive and had some chance of making a life for herself. If it wasn't already too late. Oh, God, she loved him. He was so dear. Lisan.

David ripped the piece of paper out of the type-writer, balled it up impatiently, and tossed it into the wastebasket, which was almost overflowing from this morning's fruitless production. He hadn't thought he'd be able to concentrate, and he'd been right. Most of the time he'd sat staring at the piece of blank paper like a zombie, seeing only Billie's face as it had been before he left her this morning.

It was as if she'd built a shell around herself, feverish, bright, glittering, and totally impenetrable. She wouldn't admit to anything's being in the least wrong, had laughed at her distress the night before, and insisted on his going to his apartment to work. She'd kissed him lightly and practically pushed him out the door, saying she'd see him at lunch.

Why the hell had he let her do it? He'd thought at the time that a few hours alone to think might make her more amenable to confiding in him. God knows he didn't want to force the issue, when he could feel the pain that was sheltered behind that wall. Now he wasn't sure it had been wise to delay the confrontation. It might just give the wound time to fester. She had to talk to him, dammit! He had a gut feeling about what the problem was, but he couldn't solve it unless she brought it out in the open.

There was a knock on the door, and at his terse "Come in," it was opened by Karim.

"Sit down, Karim," David said wearily, gesturing to the cane chair. "I'm sorry I didn't let you know that I wouldn't pin you for breakfast."

Karim dropped into the chair, his white robe billowing slightly. "It doesn't matter," he said haltingly, his manner oddly awkward. "I was just a little concerned. Is Miss Callahan feeling better?"

"I think you knew she was never really sick." David's eyes met his steadily. "And no, I don't think she's really very much better. I just gave up trying to talk to her for the time being."

"Shareen?" At David's nod, the sheikh's face became thoughtful. "She's such a little warrior, I wouldn't expect her to back down like that when facing a rival. It's very puzzling."

"But it wasn't Shareen she was really facing." David leaned back tiredly in his chair. "It was ghosts from the past, and they can be as hard as the devil to fight."

There was a flicker of relief on Karim's face. "I'm glad it wasn't my bringing Shareen here that troubled her." His smile was bittersweet. "We all have to face our own ghosts. Perhaps she'll find that the phantoms tend to dissolve when we put the sword of reality to them."

"Perhaps," David said. "Lord, I hope so." He smiled wryly. "Provided I can make her stand still long enough to admit they actually exist."

"If there's something I can do to help . . ."

"No, nothing." David's lips twisted. "You're very concerned about Billie. Have you finally decided she's not out to murder me?"

"It would seem unlikely," Karim said gruffly. "I have had to become a keen judge of character over the years. From what I've seen in the past two weeks, she has much too soft a heart to make a successful criminal."

"At last," David said. "I tried to tell you that the first day I brought her here. I wouldn't say your judgment—"

There was a knock on the door, and Yasmin opened it without invitation. There was a worried frown on her face, but David failed to notice it. His eyes were on the two objects she held in her hands. A tape recorder and one slightly battered guitar.

"She's gone, Lisan," Yasmin said breathlessly. "She said she had a headache and wanted to be alone. When I came to see if she wanted lunch, she was gone." She looked at her hands. "There was only the guitar and a farewell note to me."

"And the tape recorder," David said dully. God, he never should have left her this morning. He'd seen the desperation in her. Maybe he'd been afraid to confront it.

Yasmin nodded. "She said in her note that there was a message on it for you." She held out the guitar. "This is for you."

He reached out and took the guitar, moving slowly, as if he were an old man. "Honorable Patches." It meant a great deal to her, but right now it didn't help to know that. It didn't bring her back.

"What?" Karim's brow creased in puzzlement.

"Nothing," David said numbly, setting the tape recorder on the desk. "Nothing at all."

"Would you like us to leave?" Karim asked, his usually fierce eyes gentle.

"No, it doesn't matter." He drew a deep breath and braced himself before leaning forward to switch on the recorder.

Billie's voice flowed into the room, and it gave him a little shock. It was as if she were right next to him.

"I'm sorry, David. I didn't break my promise. I tried to stay. But I can't." There was a pause before her voice came again, very husky now. "It's not because I don't love you. I do." She laughed shakily. "I've never told you that, have I? That ought to prove what a coward I am. I've loved you for such a long time and I couldn't admit it. It would have

made everything too real. But I want to say it now."
The words were a mere breath. "I love you, Lisan."

There was a muffled sob from Yasmin.

"I've left you my old friend and something else.
It's not one of mine; I can't seem to think straight
enough to put two words together right now. It's by
Roger Whittaker, but it tells it all." There was a little pause, and then the soft chords of the guitar.
Billie's voice was sweet and low, with only an occasional tremor as it soared into the room.

*You're so quiet when those around you need to
  speak*
So tranquil with the world but never meek
You laugh when any other man would cry
*You tell the truth although you know it would be
  easier to lie*

You're so beautiful inside, See you shine
*Like the sun that lights my darkness, See you
  shine*
*You're my warm after the cold, You're my youth
  when I grow old*
You're my star up there in heaven, See you shine
See you shine, see you shine, see you shine

Too deep to let this shallow world destroy
Your inner ever-burning loving joy
Too generous to think before you give
And loving life, you help all those around you live

See you shine, see you shine, see you shine.

The last words weren't quite as steady as the others, and a long silence followed. "Good-bye, David.
Thank you for all the laughter and the miracles."

Then there was only the mechanical whir of the tape. David reached out and switched off the machine.

He could feel an unfamiliar burning mist in his eyes, and for a moment he couldn't do anything but stare blindly down at the guitar in his hands. Then he pushed the chair back, stood up, and headed determinedly toward the dressing room. As he reached Karim, he thrust the guitar at him. "Hold on to this for me, will you?" A moment later he was back, carrying a small brown leather suitcase, which he tossed on the bed and opened swiftly.

"You're going after her?" Karim asked quietly.

"You're damn right I am." David was crossing the room to the rosewood armoire and pulling shirts and trousers haphazardly from the hangers. "She said she was confused, and I'm not about to let her stay that way. If she thinks I'll take that blasted guitar instead of her, she's out of her mind. I *need* her."

"And I think she needs you," Karim said heavily. "I can't say I understand these sentimental passions. I never knew a woman who moved me in that way." He shrugged. "Still, she is a woman with great spirit. Perhaps she is worth such devotion."

"She is, Karim," David said, throwing the clothes carelessly into the suitcase. "Believe me, she is."

"You will bring her back?" Yasmin asked.

"I hope so," David said soberly. "If not, I'll go with her. Either way, she's got to learn that it's the two of us together from now on." The phone on the bedside table rang stridently. "Will you get that, Karim? I want to finish packing."

Karim set the guitar down, stood up, and moved

the few feet to the bedside table. He picked up the phone and, after identifying himself, listened for a few moments. His impassive face revealed none of the shock he was experiencing. "I'll tell him, Clancy." He replaced the receiver quietly.

He turned to David. "I think you'd better stop packing, David," he said slowly. "That was Clancy. He just got a report on the mobile phone from the guard he assigned to follow Billie." He paused. "It's almost certain Ladram has her."

David felt his stomach knot with icy fear. "What the hell do you mean, 'almost certain'? Doesn't he know?"

"From what he observed, it seems highly probable. Billie was driving the Jeep through the market when her way was suddenly blocked by a sidewalk vendor. While she was waiting for him to pass, a short, stocky man in a tan burnoose jumped into the seat beside her. He made a gesture and the sidewalk vendor trundled his cart out of the way. Then Billie drove on through Zalandan to the city gates."

"If he was close enough to see all that happening, why the hell didn't he stop it?" David's face was white with anger. Short and stocky. Ladram was short and stocky, almost pudgy. "He was supposed to guard her, dammit!"

"The man was sitting very close to her," the sheikh said quietly. "Since Danilo could tell she was shocked when the man jumped into the Jeep, it would seem likely he'd have had to threaten her to get her to drive on. Danilo didn't want to risk getting Billie killed if there was a knife in her ribs."

A knife in Billie's ribs. David had a sudden vision of the atrocities Ladram had described with such relish in those letters. Billie and Ladram. He felt the bile rise in his throat and smoldering anger beginning to burn away the fear. "Where was the guard calling from?"

"He'd just reached the city gates himself. He said Billie and Ladram appeared to be heading toward the canyons. He didn't want to follow too closely in case Ladram noticed him. It's not the easiest thing in the world to trail someone unobserved in the desert."

"What if he loses them?" David asked tersely. "He may be so cautious he'll let that crazy pervert get away."

"He won't do that. Clancy says Danilo is a very good man. He has orders to follow them to Ladram's hideout and then report back to us."

"And then we go after them," David said grimly.

"No, then we wait."

"Wait for what?" David asked fiercely. "Wait until Ladram starts to send me pieces of Billie in a box? Hell, no. I'm getting her away from him."

"If we go running in there, even with a commando force, we're likely to get Billie killed. Clancy has the right idea. We wait for Ladram to contact us and then we set a trap."

"*If* he contacts us," David said bitterly. "He may decide to exact a little revenge on her to amuse himself, and go after me later."

"I don't think so." Karim's narrowed eyes were shrewd. "He's getting very impatient. I think he only wants to use her as a hostage to get you."

That made sense, but David didn't want to think of the consequences if Karim was wrong. It frightened him too much. Billie, oh, dear God, Billie.

"You will get her back, Lisan." Yasmin's voice was low and comforting. "We will all help return her to you."

"I hope to heaven you're right, Yasmin," he said wearily. His eyes fell on the guitar propped against the cane chair, and he moved slowly to pick it up before dropping back into the desk chair. The smooth wood felt warm, almost alive, under his hands. It *was* alive for Billie. Her old friend. He leaned back in the chair and held Billie's old friend close as he prepared to endure the wait.

Nine

"He won't come, you know," Billie said desperately. "Why do you think I was leaving Zalandan? We've quarreled and decided to go our own ways." She glared at him defiantly. "There's no way he's going to walk into your hands just to save my neck. He couldn't care less about me."

"So you say, luv." The thick cockney accent was almost soothing. Alphie Ladram held up the small likeness of the giraffe he was carving and appraised it with narrowed eyes. "We'll just have to see, won't we? It shouldn't be long until we know one way or the other. It's almost sunset, and Bradford should be meeting my man at the city gates now. Another forty-five minutes and he should be here."

"He won't be here, I tell you. He knows what you want to do to him. He'd be a fool to come here."

"But he'll be here anyway." Ladram looked up, and there was a flicker of malice in the flat gray eyes. Serpent's eyes. It was the first hint of emotion she had seen him exhibit since he'd jumped into the Jeep with her early this morning. "He *is* a fool in some ways. He thinks he's some bloomin' Galahad. That's why he stuck his nose in what didn't concern him in the first place. He'll come, all right."

Yes, he would. She knew he would, and it was sending her into a frenzy of terror. He'd come and Ladram would kill him and it would be all her fault. David would die because she'd been too much of a coward to stay and take whatever life and love had to offer. Oh, God, she'd give anything for the chance to do that now. What did it matter if it didn't last forever? The memory alone would be precious enough to last her a lifetime. But David might not have any time at all now. Not if Ladram had his way. She tugged once more at the ropes securing her wrists in front of her, but it was futile. The bonds were so tight they were practically cutting off her circulation.

"You're uncomfortable? What a pity," Ladram said silkily, his ebullient smile making him resemble an innocent cherub. "Never fear, Galahad will be here soon to rescue you." He leaned lazily back against the boulder that faced the opening of the cave. "That will be a jolly treat for all of us, luv."

Now that he'd discarded the burnoose, she could see how squat was his square body. He was almost plump, and his thinning red hair made a fiery contrast with his pale, freckled face. His appearance had been a complete shock to her. Whenever she'd thought of Ladram in the past weeks, she'd thought of someone thin, dark, and lethal as a panther. This cockney cherub with the flat, emotionless eyes of a snake was both less and more menacing than she'd imagined. There was no question that menace existed, however. It was easily seen in those dead eyes.

"Why run the risk of killing David? You know how everyone in the Ben Raschid family feels about him. They'll hunt you down like a wild animal."

"But you don't understand," Ladram said softly. "That's what I am now. An animal on the run. Everything I've scrounged and worked for since I was a lad in Liverpool is gone. There's only one thing left now." He looked down at the sharp, glittering blade in his hand. "Pretty, isn't it? It's come a long way with me from the docks in Liverpool." He looked up to smile with such lethal ferocity that she shivered. "It has only a little farther to go."

"They'll follow David and your accomplice and capture you anyway," Billie argued. "If you leave right now, you might get away before they get here."

"How kind of you to warn me," Ladram said lightly. "Such a considerate lass. I can see why Bradford was so taken with you." His knife moved carefully over the giraffe, and a thin curl of wood drifted to the stony floor of the cave. "He won't be followed. Dion has orders to be quite sure no one's trailing them before he leaves the city. If he's followed, he's to leave Bradford and come straight here to tell me." He smiled gently. "And then I will proceed to cut your throat, Miss Callahan."

She inhaled sharply. There was no question of his sincerity. It was all there in those cold gray eyes.

"No, he won't be followed," Ladram said. "But just to make sure, Dion will stay down at the bottom of the cliff, guarding the trail that leads up to the cave." His knife shaved another fine curl.

"Then there will be just the three of us up here together. Won't that be cozy, luv?"

The picture he painted was enough to make her feel sick. David alone and without a weapon, and Ladram with that needle-sharp knife. The thought sent a cold, wracking shudder through her. "Please," she whispered, "I'll do anything. Just don't hurt him."

"Are you trying to tempt me with your fair young body?" Ladram's lips curled in amusement. "I don't want to put down your somewhat meager charms, but you've no bargaining power there. I don't fancy women very much."

"I didn't mean that," Billie said, trying to keep the anger out of her voice. "I didn't think a man who used women as you did would."

"Then, we don't have anything to talk about, do we? Why don't you just be quiet and relax? It shouldn't be long."

He settled himself more comfortably, his eyes fixed on the entry of the cave with the anticipation of a little boy expecting a treat.

Billie closed her eyes and drew a deep, shaky breath, but she could still see Ladram's face before her. From the appearance of the cave—the sleeping bag, the heap of empty food cans in the corner—Ladram had been occupying this cave not fifteen miles from Zalandan for a number of days. He'd been weaving his web of vengeance like a malevolent spider and just waiting for his prey to become entangled in it. The treat he expected was David served up on a silver platter ready for the carving knife. She wouldn't be able to stand it if he hurt David. Oh, please, don't come, Lisan. Don't come!

She opened her eyes, and her gaze compulsively followed Ladram's to the wide opening of the cave.

The sky was already tinted with delicate streaks of pink. Soon it would be the blazing scarlet of sunset. David would be meeting Ladram's cohort now, and she knew he wouldn't disobey Ladram's instructions and chance getting her killed. No, he'd do just as Ladram said, and come alone and unarmed up the winding trail from the foot of the cliff and into this cave . . . where Ladram waited with his smile of anticipation, his cold eyes, and his wickedly sharp knife.

Dressed in black jeans and a black Windbreaker, he stood quietly at the mouth of the cave, with the last brilliant rays of the setting sun behind him. She had a fleeting memory of that night in the greenhouse. He'd been all in black that night too. Its somber darkness had made him look so vibrantly golden and alive. Alive.

Ladram rose slowly to his feet. "Welcome, Bradford," he said genially. "We've been waiting for you very eagerly, haven't we, Miss Callahan? She was trying to convince me you wouldn't come, but I knew you would. You're such a gallant man, out to save the whole world and all the poor unfortunates in it. How could you resist the plight of a pretty little woman like her?"

David's gaze was running anxiously over Billie's bound form, seated against the wall of the cave. "Are you okay, Billie? Did he hurt you?"

She shook her head. "I'm not hurt," she said huskily. "You shouldn't have come, David. God, I was hoping you wouldn't come."

"I had to," he said, a little smile curving his lips. "I don't know how to play that guitar. I need you to teach me." He repeated softly, "I need you."

She felt a rush of love so poignant and intense

that it made her breathless. "I need you too," she whispered.

"Very touching," Ladram said mockingly. He tossed aside the wooden figure he'd been whittling, but kept the knife in his hand. "And I need you, too, Bradford. It's been a burning so long inside me that it's almost a passion. I dream about you every night, do you know that? All I can think about is how I want to mutilate that handsome face of yours." His hand ran caressingly over the blade of the knife. "For a start, that is."

"No!" Billie struggled desperately to her feet, using the wall of the cave to push herself forward. "You can't do that."

"You don't want his face spoiled?" Ladram smiled. "I'm always willing to oblige a lady. I'll start somewhere else first. Come closer, Bradford. I want to choose my points."

David hesitated and then came slowly forward until he stood only a few feet away from Ladram. "You see how obedient he is?" Ladram shot her a mocking glance. "That's because of you, Miss Callahan. He knows if he resists doing whatever I wish with him, I'll start on you instead. Such a gallant man." His eyes were running hungrily over David's body. "Now, let's see. Where do I begin?"

"Please." Billie moved forward impulsively. "That's not the way to hurt him most." Her voice was low and shaking. "You want to punish him. You want to make him suffer for a long time, right? What you have in mind would be over much too soon."

"Would it, now?"

She nodded, her frantic words tumbling over one another. "There's another way. You're right. He does care about me. He cares very much. What-

ever you have in mind for him, do to me instead."
She heard David's sharp exclamation, but she
ignored it. She had to convince Ladram. "Make
him watch it and then set him free. Can't you see
that would hurt him more? He'd carry the picture
for the rest of his life." But, she thought, David
would be *alive*.

"Damn it, Billie, shut up!" David said, his voice
sharp with agony. "For God's sake, keep out of
this."

"It's all my fault," Billie said fiercely. "How can I
stay out of it?" She turned back to Ladram. "You
said he was the Galahad type. My way he'd remember and suffer a lot longer than yours. Can't you
see that?"

"You may be right," Ladram said slowly. He was
studying David's white, set face. "He certainly
appears to care for you."

"You know you're only playing," David said
harshly. "Cut her loose and send her away. Let's
get on with it."

"Not yet. I think we'll let her watch a bit of it." He
shot a glance at Billie. "Shall we tie him up and
begin, luv?" He moved within inches of David, who
didn't flinch. He touched the knife to David's
breast, applying just enough pressure so that it
hurt, but did not pierce the flesh.

"No!" Billie gasped. She dashed in between
them, and suddenly everything was a blur of
impressions—Ladram's surprised, then furious,
face . . . David's low exclamation behind her . . .
then a white-hot pain in her upper arm. Strange
that it should be hot, when the blade looked so
cold.

"Billie!" She dimly heard David's agonized cry,
but it was a world away. She was thrust from

between them with lightning swiftness, and stumbled to her knees. It appeared as if David moved in slow motion as he grabbed Ladram's knife hand in a bone-crushing grip, while his other hand swung forward in a slap that connected with Ladram's throat. It seemed a comparatively light blow, but Ladram's eyes immediately glazed over, and he slumped forward, unconscious. She stared dazedly at his stocky figure, lying limp only a few feet away. It was all over so quickly. David was safe. She couldn't seem to comprehend it. David was safe now.

He was kneeling beside her, and she was in his arms. The blood, she thought hazily, and tried to draw back. "No, I'll get you bloody."

"Shut up," he said brokenly. "Shut up, love."

He drew a deep breath and pushed her away from him. He retrieved the knife Ladram had dropped when he fell. Swiftly, he cut the ropes binding her wrists, then tossed the knife aside. His hands quickly unbuttoned her yellow blouse and pushed it aside to examine the knife wound. "It's only a graze in the fleshy part of your arm," he said with relief. He pulled a white handkerchief from his pocket and pressed it to the freely flowing wound. "Lord, we were lucky. He could just as well have killed you." He placed his hand over the makeshift bandage. "Hold that for a minute. I've got to get some help for you." He stood up, strode to the mouth of the cave, and waved his arms three times in a wide arc to someone in the canyon below. He was back at her side in seconds, and his expression signaled his anxiety as he noticed the paleness of her cheeks. He muttered a low curse as he dropped to his knees again and drew her carefully into his arms, one hand holding the compress firm. "You're an idiot, Billie Callahan," he said thickly. "A loving, glorious, brave idiot, but an idiot all the same. What the hell did you mean, jumping between us like that?"

She leaned against him with a contented sigh. He was so warm, and suddenly she felt so cold, icy cold. "I thought he was going to hurt you," she said wearily. "I couldn't let him do that."

"No, I guess *you* couldn't," he said huskily, his lips brushing her temple. "But if you'd only stayed out of it, neither one of us would have been hurt. I was only waiting for an opportunity to touch him. I only had to *touch* him, Billie."

Nestling closer, she could feel his warmth, but it didn't seem to pierce the sluggish cold that was running through her veins. "I don't know what you mean."

"Clancy knew I'd be searched for weapons, so he gave me one of the charming little specialties of his security arsenal." He held up his hand to show her the handsome gold-mounted onyx ring on his index finger. "All you have to do is thumb the spring on the side and a tiny needle comes out." His lips twisted. "A needle coated with enough knockout fluid to down a rhinoceros in five seconds."

"Just like James Bond," Billie said dully. She was starting to shiver. "Who did you wave to? Ladram said there wouldn't be a chance of your being followed."

"There wasn't any need for me to be followed," David answered. "Danilo, Clancy's man, was following you and saw Ladram make his play. He was here already. After he made certain there were only Ladram and his Sedikhan stooge, he reported back by mobile phone and settled down to wait. He probably took out the man guarding the trail as soon as I was halfway up the path. He was to wait for my signal before radioing Karim and Clancy to come in by helicopter."

She felt a faint stirring of indignation. "Why was Clancy's man following me? You promised I'd be free as a bird."

"Just a precaution," he said soothingly. "I was a little afraid something might happen. I wanted you to be protected."

"I don't need protection. I can take care of . . ." Suddenly she realized how dumb she was being. She hadn't been able to protect herself in this case, and it had almost cost David his life. "I guess I did need it this time."

"It's very generous of you to admit it," David said, a thread of amusement in his voice. "You must have been more frightened than I thought."

"I was scared to death. I could see him hurting you, killing you. It was terrible."

"Shhh." He pulled her closer. "It didn't happen. We'll never have to face that threat again. It's all over."

She knew intellectually that it was all over, but she didn't know it emotionally. The menace and fear were still with her. "He was such a terrible man. Did you see his eyes? So icy. It was as if he were frozen inside." She laughed shakily. "He made me cold too. I still can't get warm."

"Can't you, Billie?" He pushed her away to gaze down at her with worried eyes. The shivering was increasing in intensity, and his lips tightened as he noticed she was even paler than before. "You'll be warm soon, I promise. Just hold on." He was unzipping his jacket with one hand, the other still holding the compress. "Where the hell are Clancy and Karim?"

"It hasn't been that long, has it?" she asked vaguely. It hadn't seemed very long since he'd waved to that man down below, but perhaps it had. She couldn't seem to think straight.

"Long enough." He put the Windbreaker around her shoulders, then drew her back into his arms. "Is that better?"

It wasn't really, but he sounded so worried, she couldn't tell him. She nodded. "Much better," she muttered. She seemed to be fading in and out of consciousness, and everything was becoming a confused jumble in her mind. The knife, Ladram, the half-carved figure of the giraffe on the ground, the guitar. The guitar? How had the guitar gotten here? Oh, yes, she remembered now. "Do you really want me to teach you how to play the guitar?"

She felt him stiffen against her. "What, love?"

"The guitar. Do you really . . . ?" She couldn't speak. There was only the cold, waiting darkness.

Ten

Sheikh Karim's fierce features were set in an expression of grudging patience when Billie next opened her eyes. He sat in the ivory-cushioned cane chair, which had been drawn close to her bed; his gaze was fixed intently on her face, as if he were mentally willing her to wake. With a personality as strong as Karim's, he just might be able to do it, Billie thought sleepily.

"Ah, you're awake," Karim growled. "It took you long enough. That idiot doctor told me I wasn't to disturb you until you woke naturally." He scowled. "Four hours!"

"Sorry," Billie said, her lips quirking. He acted as if her unconsciousness were a personal insult. She sat up in bed, flinching a little as she moved her left arm. It was neatly bandaged now. Someone—Yasmin, probably—had removed her pants and shirt, and she wore a nightgown. "You didn't have to obey him, you know. I don't know why I blacked out like that."

"Shock," Karim said. "The wound itself was nothing. I tried to tell David that at the cave, but he wouldn't believe me. He was sure you were dying from loss of blood or some kind of poison Ladram had applied to the blade of the knife." His voice was indignant. "David was raving at Clancy and me for not arriving sooner with the helicopter to get you to a doctor. It was most unlike him."

"Where is he?" Billie asked.

"The doctor ordered him out of the room after David threatened to break his neck if he let you die." Karim shook his head. "As I said, most peculiar. He was pacing outside in the hall for hours until I told him I'd order the guards to drag him to his suite if he didn't leave peaceably."

"Would you have done it?"

"Yes, of course," the sheikh said simply. "I never bluff, Miss Callahan." He stretched his legs out before him. "It wasn't good for David to be here. He was suffering even more than when he heard you'd been taken." He paused, frowned, and then said forcefully, "It upsets me exceedingly to see David suffer, Miss Callahan. That's why I chose to stay and talk to you before I sent word to him that you were awake."

"I don't like the idea of David's suffering either," she said softly. She sat up straighter, and the sheet dropped to her waist. "I think you know that."

His dark gaze was fastened in surprise on the front of her faded, high-necked nightshirt. Emblazoned in shamrock green were the words: *Kiss me, I'm Irish.* "What an extraordinary garment. Does David find that particular style erotic?"

"I don't think David's ever seen me in a nightgown," she said absently. Then, seeing the sudden flicker of amusement in his face, she rushed on. "Yasmin must have thought this old nightshirt was better for an invalid." She grinned. "She'd never have opted for such an unfeminine garment if she'd had a choice. She's always chiding me for being unwomanly."

"David seems to have no complaints on that score." The sheikh's lips curved in a little smile. "He has no complaints at all about you." His smile faded. "Except for your predilection for running away from ghosts. That was most unwise of you, Miss Callahan. David could have been murdered because of you."

"I know," Billie whispered, her lips tightening in pain as she remembered Ladram's face when he was holding that knife to David's chest. "It was horrible." Her eyes flew to his. "Where is Ladram?"

"He has been taken care of," Karim said in a harsh, implacable tone. "He won't be a problem any longer to anyone."

Billie shivered at Karim's ferocity. "I'm glad. David will be safe, at last."

"You can be sure of that," the sheikh said, "if your foolishness doesn't lead him into some other danger." His expression was stern. "I've decided that I can't permit that."

"You can't permit—"

"It's obvious you care very deeply for David," Karim interrupted. "From what he told me of what happened with Ladram, you were willing to give your life for him. It is not reasonable you should do that and then make him suffer by refusing to stay with him."

"And you intend to make sure that I don't do anything so stupidly unreasonable?" Billie's eyes were twinkling. "Am I being threatened with the eunuch guards and the harem again?" It was hard to remember how angry she'd been that first day. She was finding it difficult even to take Karim's threats seriously, knowing it was all done for the love of David. She might be pretty ruthless herself if she thought David's happiness was at stake.

"I told you I was not so uncivilized," Karim said. "But you'd be wise to take me more seriously. I have confidence in David's ability to convince you that your future happiness lies with him." His lips firmed determinedly. "I just intend to make sure that he has the time and opportunity to do so."

"Really? You sound very stern," Billie said demurely. "Would you care to elaborate?"

"I was about to do that," Karim said. "First, you will not be permitted to leave the Casbah or the city unless David accompanies you. Second, you will be moved from here into David's suite immediately. Third, I will permit no birth-control devices to be brought into the Casbah. Any that you have will be confiscated and not returned to you until I'm sure this foolishness is out of your head."

Why, that wily old devil! "Are you sure you don't want to confiscate all my shoes as well?" she asked solemnly.

"Your shoes?" Karim's thick brows were knotted in puzzlement.

"I thought it might be in order, since you obviously want to keep me barefoot and pregnant," she said silkily. "I'm surprised you haven't considered artificial insemination."

"I'm not *that* civilized," Karim said with a reluctant smile. "I believe that David will take care of the matter in an entirely natural and pleasurable manner."

"I'm sure he will," Billie said, meeting his eyes steadily. "With no interference on your part."

"We will see," Karim said. "Whatever is necessary will be done." He lifted his brow. "You don't seem too upset. You will accept your fate with fitting meekness?"

Fitting meekness! Karim had a great deal to learn about modern women and their independence. Well, now she had all the time in the world to teach him.

"I'm going to stay with David, if that's what you mean," she said as she threw aside the covers and swung her legs to the floor. "In fact, I think I'll go see him this minute. Is he in his suite?"

Karim shook his head. "He's in the greenhouse."

"Good." She found she was a little weaker than she'd expected. "Then, I'll toddle down there with 'fitting meekness' to accept my lord's decrees."

"I can send for him," Karim said. "You shouldn't be out of bed so soon."

"I want to go to him," Billie said quietly. "I was the one who ran away. It's only right that I be the one to walk the return road. It's a sort of symbol. I think David will like that. He has an appreciation for rituals."

"I think he will too." Karim rose to his feet and looked down at her with conflicting emotions on his hard, fierce face. "I'm not one to obey orders." He touched the garish slogan emblazoned across the nightshirt. "Still, there's always a first time . . . Billie." He bent and placed an awkward kiss on her forehead. "You'll find you haven't made a mistake."

She felt inexpressibly touched, and the tears misted her eyes. No wonder David loved the ferocious old brigand. She cleared her throat and gave him a cheeky grin. "I know I haven't. However, you may not be so lucky. You may just decide I'm too difficult to live with and shoo David and me back to Marasef." She strode toward the gauzy curtains at the door of the dressing room. She halted to glance back at him over her shoulder. "I think I should tell you I had made up my mind to stay." Her violet eyes were dancing. "And that your dire threats didn't mean a tinker's damn to me. If I'd wanted to, I'd have found a way to escape from the Casbah. As for the pregnancy threat"—she shrugged—"I love babies. I'd have just slung the baby on my back like an Indian and taken it with me." She disappeared through the curtain, leaving the sheikh staring after her with an expression that was a curious mixture of outrage and pride.

The path that led through the greenhouse was as mystically lovely as before, the moonlight lending a crystal purity to the flowering jasmine and shimmering gold Allamanda. It should have reminded her of that first night, but somehow it didn't. That evening had been all magic and dreams, and tonight was sweet, vibrant life and reality. She could feel the life zinging through her veins and its rhythm springing in her footsteps. Tonight she could almost hear the other rhythms of the earth and nature surrounding her. Perhaps, given time, David would be able to transmit that wondrous empathy to her.

He was kneeling by the bed of pinks and wind-flowers, as she'd known he would be, the lantern beside him, as it had been on that evening that seemed so long ago. So alike, yet so different. His hands weren't working busily in the earth; they were jammed tensely into the pockets of his black

Windbreaker, and his eyes were staring blindly at the healthy green sprigs in the earth before him.

"They've grown quite a bit since you planted them, haven't they?" she asked in a low voice.

He jerked around to face her, his eyes wide and startled. "Billie! What are you doing here? Why aren't you in bed?"

She crossed the few feet that separated them and dropped to her knees beside him. "You don't sound very welcoming," she said with a little smile. "I'm not in bed because I don't want to be. And I'm here because that's where you are." Her eyes twinkled. "Karim told me you were so objectionable, he had to banish you."

"You wouldn't wake up," he said simply. "I didn't know what to do." He suddenly reached out and pulled her into his arms, burying his face in her hair. "Oh, God, you're all right! I was so afraid you might die."

Her arms went around his waist to hold him fiercely to her. She laughed shakily. "From that scratch? No way. I just swooned in a very idiotic and womanly fashion. Yasmin would have been proud of me."

"But you wouldn't wake up," David said stubbornly. "That damn doctor wouldn't even let me try to wake you." His arms tightened. "I wanted to *know*."

"Well, you know now," she said soothingly, with maternal tenderness. "Could I have walked all this way if I wasn't fine?"

"I guess not," he muttered. "You shouldn't have done it. I told Karim to send for me."

"That's what he said, but I wouldn't let him. I wanted to come to you." She leaned back in his arms to smile up at him. "My own little ritual."

"What ritual?"

One hand left his shoulder to reach down and gently stroke one of the green sprigs with a gentle finger. "Love." She nestled her cheek closer to him while her finger continued to caress the slender green sprig. "They're standing so much taller than when you first planted them," she said dreamily. "I had no idea they'd flourish like that."

"Just give it a chance and love will flourish wherever you plant it," David said gravely. "But you've got to give it a chance. I wasn't going to let you go, you know. I was coming after you. Those other people who danced in and out of your life may have let you go, but not me. Not ever. If you won't stay with me, then I'll trail along behind you like a faithful troubadour, carrying your guitar on my back. I'll pick grapes with you in the Napa Valley, go pearl diving in Samoa, or weave baskets for the tourists in Nassau." His sapphire eyes were glowing with an almost incandescent warmth. "We'll live together, work together, love together. And do you know what? Someday you'll find you've taken root at last, windflower. I'll be your roots, just as you'll be mine, and they'll intertwine and grow stronger through the years."

She could feel her throat tighten with tears. "But you love it here in Sedikhan. Your home is here, and all the people you love."

"Not all the people I love," he said quietly. "The one I love the most is finding it impossible to stay here." There was a flicker of pain in his eyes. "And that means I can't stay here either." His lips tenderly brushed her temple. "Who knows? I might learn to like the life of a gypsy. We'll have the laughter and the miracles wherever we are."

"Yes, we'll still have them." Her heart was swelling with such a fountain of love that it was almost painful. "It's a very pretty picture you're painting, but I'm afraid it's just not destined to come to pass."

He frowned, and his lips tightened sternly. "Look, Billie, we both know what the real problem is. You don't lightly float on the surface of life; you're running away from it. At least, you're running away from affection and commitment. So what if some stupid asses in your childhood didn't have the sense to realize what a treasure you are? That doesn't mean we're all like that. I love you, and I intend to love you for the rest of my life." He drew a deep, shaky breath. "And if there's an afterlife, even longer than that. Somewhere beyond the sun I'll still be loving you, Billie."

Somewhere beyond the sun. Yes, she'd still be loving him then too. As they passed through the exquisite rhythms and cycles of life to other spheres, it would still be with her, warming her, making her all she could be, making her part of him. If it was so with her, she could almost believe it would be that way with him too. And if it turned out it wasn't, then she'd still consider herself lucky she'd been blessed with a love so very special.

"David." Her voice was a broken murmur. "I love you so very much."

"Then, you'll let me come with you?"

She shook her head. "I told you that wasn't possible." She lowered her eyes to hide the sudden glint of mischief in them. "It just wouldn't work out."

David frowned. "Of course it would. Why the hell wouldn't it?"

"Well, this carefree, gypsy life you're talking about would be very difficult to manage," she drawled. "Seeing that Karim's going to keep me locked up in the Casbah, barefoot and pregnant." She tilted her head consideringly. "No, that's not right. I believe he was going to let me keep my shoes."

"What!"

"Karim decided to step in and keep me from making you any unhappier," she said with a little smile tugging at her lips. "I think you'll find my things have been moved into your suite when we get back. I'm under house arrest." She wrinkled her nose at him teasingly. "With you as jailer. Oh, yes, no birth-control devices until I see the light and accept you as my mate with 'fitting meekness.' "

"Oh, Lord, he didn't." David groaned, closing his eyes. "Tell me he didn't."

"He did." Billie's eyes were dancing. "For a moment or two, I practically could hear my slave bracelets jangle!"

"It's a wonder you didn't try to make a break for it on the spot." David opened his eyes to gaze at her earnestly. "He means well, sweetheart. He just doesn't know how to cope with something like this."

"I think I'll have to teach him," Billie said lightly. "I hope he's a fast learner, because I don't intend to spend the next few years tutoring him on how to treat independent, liberated womankind. I'll have too much to do reorganizing the Casbah, making sure that Yusef is married to Daina, and getting to know Alex and Bree and Honey and Lance. Then I think I'll try to do something on a professional level with those songs of mine. And of course I'll have to nag you to keep writing those beautiful books.

That's all very time-consuming, and Karim will just have to take his—"

"Billie, what are you talking about?" David interrupted sternly. "I'm not about to let you be coerced into staying here, when you don't want to. I'll have a talk with Karim and straighten all this out."

"I have straightened it all out," she said, lowering her eyes humbly. "I've resigned myself to my fate, just as Karim ordered. I'm going to sit quietly in my seraglio and wait for my lord's commands. Perhaps if I'm very good, your munificence will be so great that you'll allow a jaunt to Marasef someday." She fluttered her lashes demurely. "Of course, I realize that's a lot to ask."

"Billie, will you stop joking?" His hands tightened on her arms, and when she flinched, he dropped them as if he'd been scalded. "Damn, I'm sorry. I forgot about your wound."

"First you think I'm dying, and then you forget I've been hurt. You're not very consistent, David."

"That's because you're driving me crazy." His hands came up to cup her face, tilting it so he could look into her eyes. "Now, *talk* to me."

Her violent eyes were glowing softly with a light as radiant as the aurora borealis. "You don't know how to play the guitar. I have to teach you, remember? Since I've turned Honorable Patches out to pasture, I can't take him with me on the road, so I guess I'll just have to stick around here until you learn." She smiled teasingly. "Considering you're almost tone deaf, it shouldn't take more than the next fifty or sixty years."

Then, as she saw the dawning of joy in those sapphire eyes, she launched herself into his embrace, her arms hugging him tightly to express all the love that was bubbling up inside her. "I don't need other places, other people, David. All I need is you. For the rest of my life, all I'm going to need is you." Her voice was muffled in the curve of his shoulder. "You know those roots you were talking about? They're already there, and growing stronger every day. I realized that in the cave this afternoon. When I thought you were going to die, I knew that if you did, there wouldn't be anything left." She lifted her head to gaze steadily into his eyes. "I can't promise you I won't get scared and insecure again. I probably will. It's been ingrained in me too long to vanish overnight. I will promise that I'll never run away from you again. I'll run toward you instead." Her voice was suddenly husky. "There's nothing out there in the world for me any more that I can't have here. I used to think there was something glimmering on the horizon, just waiting for me. But it was always gone when I got there. It was like a will-o'-the-wisp, a phantom I couldn't touch." She leaned forward and kissed him with loving sweetness. "It was *you* out there waiting for me. At last I've reached that final horizon. I can touch it now, and it's more beautiful than anything that could ever be over the next hill."

"You're sure?" David asked, his eyes jewel-bright with a love that took her breath away. "Lord, I want you to be happy, my darling!"

"How could I help it?" She laughed shakily. "I have the horizon, love, and Lisan." She slowly drew his head down once more to kiss him tenderly. "Oh, yes, I have Lisan."

Their lips met while the deep, singing rhythms of the earth and a thousand living blossoms throbbed around them. She could hear them. Oh, dear, sweet heaven, she could *hear* them!

THE EDITOR'S CORNER

With the Olympic Games in Los Angeles much on our minds these past days, we remembered a letter we got last year from Barbara York of Houston, Texas. Barbara gave us a compliment that was truly heart-warming. "If there were an Olympics for category romances," she wrote, "LOVESWEPT would win all the gold medals!"

I don't know about winning them *all* (we're always impressed by the works of talented writers in our competitors' lines). I do know, though, that all our LOVESWEPT authors and staff strive constantly for excellence in our romance publishing program ... and that we love our work!

And now to the "solid gold" LOVESWEPTS you can expect from us next month.

Joan J. Domning is back with a marvelously evocative romance, **LAHTI'S APPLE,** LOVESWEPT #63. How this romance appeals to the senses. Place, time, sight, sound, tender emotion leap from the pages in this sensitive, yet passionate story of the growing love between heroine Laurian Bryant and hero Keska Lahti. A disillusioned musician, Keska has started an apple orchard and Laurian moves into his world to bring him fully alive. The fragrance of an apple orchard through its seasons ... the poignant, sometimes melancholy strains of violin and cello are delightfully interwoven with delicate strands of tension between two unforgettable lovers. **LAHTI'S APPLE** stays with you, haunts like a lovely melody.

And what a treat is in store for you in Joan Bramsch's second romance, **A KISS TO MAKE IT BETTER,** LOVESWEPT #64. There's playfulness, joy, humor in

(continued)

this charming love story of Jenny Larsen, a former nurse, and Dr. Jon McCallem. But there is another dimension to this romance—the healing power of love for two sensitive human beings hurt by life's inequities. A simply beautiful story!

Billie Green appeared at one of our teas for LOVE-SWEPT readers not long ago. A lady in the audience got up during the question and answer period with authors and said, "Billie, I love your autobiographical sketches in your books almost as much as I love the books themselves. All I've got to say is thank God for your mother!" There was a big, spontaneous round of applause. Well, that "tetched" quality Billie credits her mother with having passed on to her is present with all its whimsical and enriching power in **THE LAST HERO,** LOVESWEPT #65. Billie's heroine, Toby Baxter, is funny . . . but she's also so fragile a personality that you'll find yourself moist of eye and holding your breath. Then Jake Hammond, a dream of a hero—tender, powerful, yet with supreme control—begins to take gentle charge of Toby's life . . . to exorcise her demons. Different, dramatic, **THE LAST HERO** is a remarkable love story.

IN A CLASS BY ITSELF, LOVESWEPT #66, by Sandra Brown is aptly titled. It *is* an absolutely spellbinding, one-of-a-kind love story. Dani Quinn is one of Sandra's most lovable heroines ever. And Logan Webster has got to be the most devastatingly attractive man Sandra's ever dreamed up. That walk, that walk, that fabulous walk of Logan's. I guarantee you'll never forget it—nor any of the other elements in this breathtakingly emotional, totally sensual romance. In my judgment, **IN A CLASS BY ITSELF** is Sandra Brown's most delicious, heartwarming love story—in short, my favorite of all her books. You won't want to miss it!

You know, these four LOVESWEPTS *do* have the properties of real gold—shine and brilliance on the surface, the true and "forever" value beneath.

Hope you agree.

Warm regards,

Carolyn Nichols

Carolyn Nichols
   Editor
LOVESWEPT
Bantam Books, Inc.
666 Fifth Avenue
New York, NY 10103

WILD SWAN

Celeste De Blasis

Author of THE PROUD BREED

Spanning decades and sweeping from England's West Country in the years of the Napoleonic Wars to the beauty of Maryland's horse country—a golden land shadowed by slavery and soon to be ravaged by war—here is a novel richly spun of authentically detailed history and sumptuous romance, a rewarding woman's story in the grand tradition of A WOMAN OF SUBSTANCE. WILD SWAN is the story of Alexandria Thaine, youngest and unwanted child of a bitter mother and distant father—suddenly summoned home to care for her dead sister's children. Alexandria—for whom the brief joys of childhood are swiftly forgotten . . . and the bright fire of passion nearly extinguished.

Buy WILD SWAN, on sale in hardcover August 15, 1984, wherever Bantam Books are sold, or use the handy coupon below for ordering:

 **LOVESWEPT**

Love Stories you'll never forget by authors you'll always remember

LOVESWEPT

Love Stories you'll never forget by authors you'll always remember

☐	21630	**Lightning That Lingers #25** Sharon & Tom Curtis	$1.95
☐	21631	**Once In a Blue Moon #26** Billie J. Green	$1.95
☐	21632	**The Bronzed Hawk #27** Iris Johansen	$1.95
☐	21637	**Love, Catch a Wild Bird #28** Anne Reisser	$1.95
☐	21626	**The Lady and the Unicorn #29** Iris Johansen	$1.95
☐	21628	**Winner Take All #30** Nancy Holder	$1.95
☐	21635	**The Golden Valkyrie #31** Iris Johansen	$1.95
☐	21638	**C.J.'s Fate #32** Kay Hooper	$1.95
☐	21639	**The Planting Season #33** Dorothy Garlock	$1.95
☐	21629	**For Love of Sami #34** Fayrene Preston	$1.95
☐	21627	**The Trustworthy Redhead #35** Iris Johansen	$1.95
☐	21636	**A Touch of Magic #36** Carla Neggers	$1.95
☐	21641	**Irresistible Forces #37** Marie Michael	$1.95
☐	21642	**Temporary Forces #38** Billie Green	$1.95
☐	21646	**Kirsten's Inheritance #39** Joan Domning	$2.25
☐	21645	**Return to Santa Flores #40** Iris Johansen	$2.25
☐	21656	**The Sophisticated Mountain Gal #41** Joan Bramsch	$2.25
☐	21655	**Heat Wave #42** Sara Orwig	$2.25
☐	21649	**To See the Daisies . . . First #43** Billie Green	$2.25
☐	21648	**No Red Roses #44** Iris Johansen	$2.25
☐	21644	**That Old Feeling #45** Fayrene Preston	$2.25
☐	21650	**Something Different #46** Kay Hooper	$2.25

Prices and availability subject to change without notice.

LOVESWEPT

Love Stories you'll never forget by authors you'll always remember